The Revival at Rockville

The Revival at Rockville

JOSEPH B. ONYANGO OKELLO

RESOURCE *Publications* • Eugene, Oregon

THE REVIVAL AT ROCKVILLE

Resource Publications
An Imprint of Wipf and Stock Publishers
199 W. 8th Ave., Suite 3
Eugene, OR 97401

www.wipfandstock.com

PAPERBACK ISBN: 979-8-3852-5790-4
HARDCOVER ISBN: 979-8-3852-5791-1
EBOOK ISBN: 979-8-3852-5792-8

VERSION NUMBER 01/21/26

1

Louella Goodman was quite a self-styled florist. She built a reputation around the block, in the city of Rockville, for stocking her shop with some of the freshest flowers in town. Funeral directors, wedding planners, and partygoers routinely flocked to her shop for the most appealing ensemble of flowers for their gigs. Her rapport with customers, near and far, made her the talk of the town, indeed, its envy.

Rockville was a city of about sixty thousand people, but it was growing rapidly. The fire department was getting overwhelmed by the day-to-day demands of operation—a fire here, a medical emergency there, and, sometimes, a drowning by the nearby Rockville River whose massive width and dangerous water volume seemed to dwarf the size of the city itself. The police department seemed overwhelmed by similar demands, but they did what they could to give the citizens the impression that they were doing their work. Every election cycle, mayoral candidates would vow to increase the number of fire stations to meet the demands of the city's growing size. Once voted in, however, they focused on other priorities.

As Louella entered her shop that Friday morning, she barely settled into her daily routine before the door swung open, and in walked a well-built six-foot tall young man. His well-groomed hair fell neatly in place. His ironed shirt matched remarkably well with his pants. Louella wondered if he was from around town. He knew almost all her customers by name. He certainly made an impression on her when he walked into the shop.

"Wow," Louella thought, "He must be in his late twenties, maybe early thirties. I wonder if he is single."

She was immediately embarrassed that her mind took her in that direction. She grew up under strict Christian values. "Always shun love-at-first-sight propensities," her mother warned her incessantly. Regular church attendance was always expected. She castigated herself for dropping the ball on her feelings.

"You miss church only when you are sick and shut-in," her mother declared and was not to be talked into believing other reasons for not going to church were available.

A few more customers walked into the shop, including a mother, possibly in her late twenties, with a baby in a stroller. The baby was sucking on a light blue pacifier. Louella also noticed a silver-haired, middle-aged gentleman walking in. He seemed interested in getting a rose flower, possibly for someone significant in his life. But that was not Louella's business, she thought. Her business was to sell flowers and to sell them quickly before they withered in her shop. The silver-haired gentleman paused to look at a few more floral arrangements on the shelves. He seemed to acknowledge the well-built young man's presence in the shop with a nod, a smile, and a remark that Louella could not understand. The well-built young man laughed at whatever the middle-aged man said and kept checking out the flowers he needed. But the silver-haired gentleman walked out as abruptly as he came in. The young mother, however, was still inside the building.

"Excuse me, ma'am," asked the well-built young man. "Do you have any fresh flowers today?"

"The stock I have is yesterday's," she replied. "A new consignment is on the way. It should be here pretty soon. You can come back later, perhaps in an hour."

"Oh, okay," the young man replied. "Let me run some errands at the post office and bank. I can then stop by just to see if they'll be here by then."

"You know . . ."

"Sam. The name's Sam Palmer," said the young man as he stretched out his hand to shake Louella's. Louella was taken aback by his firm grip when Sam shook her hand.

"My goodness! What a grip you've got there!" she said. "Are you a trainer or something?"

"Not really," answered Sam. "I go to the local fitness gym two blocks from here."

"Nice!"

"I could train you if you want, though!"

Louella's heart almost skipped a beat at the thought of getting trained by this handsome, well-built young man.

Still, she asked, "But what do you do for a living, then?"

"I'm a wedding planner," he responded.

"Of course," Louella replied. "That explains why you stopped by here. You know what," she went on, "let me call the delivery company to see how long it will take to get the next stock in."

"Suit yourself," Sam said as Louella picked up the phone to make the call. Meanwhile, Sam paced up and down the shop, looking at some of the flowers by the shelves, hanging delicately off some hooks while others sat gingerly in vases placed on shelves inside a refrigerator. Sam wondered how long some of the flowers had been sitting there before Louella's voice interrupted his thoughts.

"Oh, you guys are almost here?" Louella half asked, half exclaimed. "Wonderful! I'll meet you outside," she said.

The van came in and the delivery man began offloading the flowers into Louella's shop as she delicately placed them in different vases. Then she remembered Sam. Sam? Where was he? Sam was on the floor looking for his pen, which had dropped out of his hands and rolled under one of the steel shelves in the shop.

"There you are!" he said as if the pen could hear him. He then stood up straight to find Louella looking curiously at him, wondering how he ended up on the floor.

"I was trying to pull my pen out of my pocket to make a list of the types of flowers I would be needing. But the sneaky pen fell right through my fingers."

"Come over," Louella said, "and I will help you get what you need." The service was quick and efficient. Louella had mastered the art. She got him his flowers and sent him on his way.

"Please come and see us again," said Louella, desperately hoping Sam would return so she could get to know him better.

She worked all day. Some hours did have heavy traffic in her shop. Others were uneventful. Louella took the time to take stock of what flowers she had left during those downtimes. Occasionally she checked her email, then her Facebook account, back to her email, then to Instagram. She saw nothing new there except for a few political comments about the next campaign in town. As she looked intently into the list of stock she had, the sound of the phone ringing made her jump.

"Hello," she said.

"Hi, Louella. It's Sam. I just got home. I was wondering if you and I could go out for a cup of coffee after you shut down this evening."

Louella could not believe her luck. But she tried to hide her excitement. Not only was she floored by the fact that she was talking to Sam. She was elated that Sam was asking her out on a date. Something inside her screamed at her to say yes. A more reasonable voice counseled her to hide her excitement and not look too eager to accept the offer.

"Hi, Sam! So nice to hear you again. Let me see. I believe my evening is open. I can meet you at the . . ."

"Town House Coffee, perhaps," Sam offered.

"Town House Coffee? Where is that?" Louella asked.

"It's down by Second Street, very close to Jones Bank," Sam answered. "You can't miss it. It's the only green-roofed building on that street."

"I know where Jones Bank is. I'll come right over when I close."

Strangely, for Louella, time seemed to slow down. She kept looking at the clock, but it seemed to mock her with its snail's pace. Finally, the clock struck five, and Louella shut down her business. After making sure all her books were in order and the next day's stock were set to arrive at 8 am, she locked the door, walked to her car, threw her purse in the passenger's seat, and sped off to Town House Coffee.

2

Downtown Rockville was quite an experience with different sorts of restaurants, malls, boutiques, and fitness centers. The list seemed endless. The streets were beehives of activity. Everyone seemed in a hurry to get somewhere except for the handfuls of homeless individuals sitting by different intersections, trying to get the attention of anyone willing to drop a few coins into their outstretched hands.

As Louella maneuvered through the slightly heavy traffic, she shifted from one lane to another, trying to slot herself into any space she could find ahead of her. She wanted to get to the coffeehouse as quickly as she could but was getting frustrated by the red lights she seemed to encounter at every intersection. Moreover, the traffic on either side of her seemed to go faster than her lane, that is until she moved to the faster lane. Then everything seemed to stop. The honking and revving engines made the insanity worse than it was.

Finally, she could see it, the bright red neon lights reading, "Town House Coffee," with a "Yes, We Are Open" sign by the door. It seemed too welcoming to ignore. As her heart kept pounding, she was not sure whether this date meant the beginning of a new phase of life. Her previous relationship was not what she was looking for. Thankfully, her breakup with Truett, her former boyfriend, was not as painful as it could have been. Both remained friends and checked on each other's welfare. However, Truett moved out of town due to a career change. That move was something Louella was not anticipating when Truett broke the news to her the first time he knew about it, which is why they broke up, both wishing the other all the best.

Louella finally found a convenient parking spot, turned off the engine, stepped out of the car, and walked into the restaurant. As she opened the door, one waitress greeted her with a smile.

"Welcome to Town House Coffee," she said. "Will this be for one?"

"For two please," Louella replied. "In fact," she went on, "he might be here. His name is Sam!"

"Oh! Sam! He's already here. Come on this way."

As she followed the waitress, Louella saw Sam sitting in a corner booth, working on a Sudoku puzzle. Their walk seemed loud enough to get Sam's attention. He looked up and smiled.

"Louella," he said, half excitedly and half approvingly, "that was fast of you. How did you weave through traffic that quickly?"

"Oh, it was not heavy at all, except for a few snarl-ups here and there. Nothing I couldn't handle. Have you placed your order?" she asked.

"Not really. I was waiting for you. What would you like?"

"Well, coffee would be nice, but I've got to look at the menu for their chewables."

"Their Danish pastry is really good," Sam offered. "You might need to give it a try."

"Hey guys! Welcome to Town House Coffee," came the voice of a waitress who listened patiently to their conversation until they paused to look at the menu. "I will be your waitress tonight. Our pound cake is really good, and we have a few specials tonight you might want to check out."

Louella, however, said, "I will just have a cup of coffee with a slice of banana bread."

"Really?" Sam asked. "Why not try something unique like, say, their coffee cake? It's really good."

"If I must," Louella surrendered.

"Get her some coffee cake. I'll have the same with a cup of coffee, too!" said Sam.

"Okay. Coming right up!"

As she walked away, Louella gave the room a quick glance. The brick wall gave it a unique ambiance. One could not imagine how else it could have looked if not this way. It was one of those houses whose walls seem to describe its name rather than the other way around. She saw several empty tables. A quick estimate led her to think the restaurant was about two-thirds full, though she noticed the same waitress leading a few more customers to their tables. As she glanced around the room, Sam interrupted her thoughts.

"So," he started. "How long have you been running your business?"

"I have done this for three years now, though I wish I had started earlier."

"Really? Why do you say that?"

"It's paying my bills with lots more besides. I like it," she went on.

"That is super. I envy you."

"So," Louella asked. "Do you have a family here? Have you always lived in Rockville?"

"As a matter of fact," Sam answered, "I moved to Rockville about six months ago from Lockridge, which, as you know, is not too far from here."

"How long have you been a wedding planner?"

"I just started. It's something I'm trying out. I'll stay on it if I like it and if it works."

"So, what did you do before then?"

"I was a bank teller. I guess that's why I referenced my gym with a bank when I stopped by at your shop."

"So, you do know something about finances? I could use a financial planner, you know."

"Not really. It was hit-and-miss. I just didn't do well there, so I changed careers."

"I hear you," Louella said. "But you didn't tell me whether or not you have family here."

"My family is back in Lockridge. I grew up there. I never really met my dad. But my mom still lives there. I stop by there from time to time."

"Ah! I see," said Louella, except Sam was not telling her what she wanted to know, and she didn't know how to ask.

"But," she went on, "Are you seeing someone at this time?" Louella was surprised by her directness, possibly even appalled. She couldn't believe she'd asked him that question.

"No, I'm not!" He said. "My last relationship didn't quite work out. She's back in Lockridge, and I decided to move down here to start afresh."

Louella's heart was pounding. Perhaps this was her chance. She looked at Sam and wondered if he could be the one. She was still unsure, but the thought of having such a well-built man in her life seemed to excite her.

"So, are you actively looking, or are you letting the process play itself out, you know like spilled water finding its own level?"

"More of the latter than the former," he said.

"I think that's wise," Louella said. "You never know what you might find."

The conversation moved on to other things—politics, sports, international issues, movies, and their religious affiliations. Louella learned that Sam used to go to church but had lost interest in it. As they talked, they weren't aware of how much time had passed.

"I'm sorry guys, but we have to close," said the waitress as she cleaned the tables next to them.

"What? Time's up?" asked Sam, quite surprised. "We barely just began. I had no clue time had gone so quickly."

Louella also realized she had enjoyed Sam's company. Sam asked Louella if she'd like to meet again at the same venue. He didn't need to ask twice.

"Yes! Let's do it again. I would love to hear more of your stories."

They both shook hands, not sure whether the gesture could graduate to a quick embrace. They said their goodbyes, but Sam offered to walk Louella to her car.

"It's late in the evening, you know," he said. "And we do have some really bad guys out there. I want to be sure you're safe."

Louella was thankful to Sam for his kind gesture. When Sam was sure she was safely seated in her car, he turned around and walked toward his truck. Only a few more cars remained in the parking lot. He found his truck, hopped in, and turned the ignition key, but nothing happened. He tried again. It choked and finally revved to life, and soon he was heading in the exact opposite direction that Louella seemed to have gone. He thought it was a good evening.

3

LOUELLA'S DRIVE HOME WAS short, possibly fifteen minutes at the most. She played out her entire conversation with Sam in her mind. She enjoyed that evening. Once again, she wondered if Sam would be the man for her. Perhaps she was rushing too quickly into a relationship. But then again, perhaps she was too slow. She was unsure. As she thought of what they discussed throughout the night, she found herself pulling into her driveway. She opened the garage door and slowly parked her car, got out, lowered the garage door, and walked into the house.

As she did, she turned off the security system and checked to see if any package had been dropped by her front door. She saw a package lying gently on the doormat. She picked it up and opened it, not sure she could remember what she'd ordered. As she opened it, she nearly kicked herself. Of course, she remembered it. She had run out of detergent, and Sam's Club had just made a delivery she purchased online three days before.

She then turned on her TV to catch up with the news. As she went through her house to ensure everything was just as she had left it, she decided to prepare herself for bed. Her phone buzzed as she went to the bathroom. It was Sam, checking to ensure she had reached home safely.

"This man is something," She thought to herself. Truett wasn't like this. Louella believed that Sam cared about her. But her mother had warned her numerous times in the past.

"If a man wants you, he will do everything he can to get you," Mom said. Perhaps this was in keeping with Mom's observation, Louella thought. Could she trust Sam? Could Sam be the kind of man with whom she wanted to spend the rest of her life? She wasn't sure about it. The more she thought about Sam, the more curious she was about him.

Louella wished she could find out more about Sam. Perhaps she could look him up on Facebook and see what kind of profile he had. He might be the kind of man who puts up a front to hide his real nature. On the other hand, he seemed very well polished and on top of his game in carrying out a conversation. He was so sure of himself. That was the kind of man Louella wanted in her life.

"Oops!" she muttered to herself. She had just admitted she was ready to take this relationship to the next level. Her thoughts kept swirling as she got ready for bed. After cleaning her teeth and jumping into her sleepwear, she youthfully bounced into her bed, pulled the blanket over her shoulders, dimmed the lights, and watched the last episode of her favorite talk show. Before she knew it, she was sleeping soundly.

"Hi, Louella!" she looked behind her, and Sam was reaching out to shake her hand. She turned around and extended hers, but it graduated to an embrace.

"Sam!" She asked, "What are you doing here?"

"Oh! I thought you needed me to help you with your package—the one you picked up at your door."

"Are you stalking me?" she asked, sounding both fearful and angry.

"No, I'm not. I just want to be sure you're safe."

There was something genuine in his voice with this remark, but Louella thought she needed to be a little more cautious. She wondered how Sam had entered her house. To her dismay, mixed with excitement, Sam leaned over to her and tried to kiss her on the lips. She pushed him aside but then regretted doing so.

Then she said, "Wait! Don't you think you're moving too quickly here?" Her voice woke her up. She was breathing heavily. It was all a dream. She got up, paced up and down her bedroom, and checked her door locks again just to be sure everything was okay. Then she checked her security system one more time before going back to bed.

Presently, she found herself on her knees. She had not done so in a long time. That night, though, in light of her date and her dream, she believed she needed to talk to her Lord about the happenings. Her mother had taught her about a Bible verse from Proverbs 3:5–6: "Trust in the Lord with all your heart and lean not on your understanding. In all your ways acknowledge him and he will direct your paths." She thought she needed to trust in the Lord a little more than she had been doing. For the first time in a long time, Louella found herself talking to her God in a way she'd never done before.

"Guide me through this uncertainty, Lord," she said, "so I may know what to do." That was her prayer repeatedly. It wasn't a crisis, but she needed to place it in God's hands. She then jumped into her bed and slept like a baby.

4

The sun's rays pierced through the blinds of Louella's bedroom window, exposing the otherwise invisible particles floating randomly in the air. It was Saturday morning, and Louella was still asleep, somewhat exhausted from the previous day's activities. The sound of her landline ringing startled her. She moved her hand sleepily over the bedside table with her eyes shut as she tried to pick up the phone.

"Hello," she said.

"Louella," came the voice at the other end of the line. "It's Pastor Matthew Roberts. Did I call at a bad time?"

"Oh! Hi, Pastor,"Louella answered. "How are you? We can talk. How can I help you?"

"Would you care to do the Scripture reading tomorrow?" Pastor Matthew went on, "I had asked Jeremy Jones last Sunday to do it for me tomorrow, but he just called to say he's come down with something, possibly the flu, and can't do it."

Louella wasn't planning to go to church that weekend, but since the pastor himself had called, she knew she had to give him the impression that she was planning to be in church. Still, she wasn't sure she had a good reading voice for public speaking, let alone reading. The pastor was still waiting at the other end of the line for her answer, and she knew she had to say something quickly.

"Of course, I will," she said, "What's your text?"

The pastor said, "It's gonna be,. . . it's gonna be,. . . wait a minute. Let me be sure of the verses. Ah! Here it is! It's gonna be Mark 1:29–34, where Jesus healed Simon Peter's mother-in-law and where he healed many more people thereafter."

"Okay," Louella said, "I'll look at it. Do you mind if I read it in the King James Version?" she asked.

"Not at all," he replied, "though my version of choice is the New Living Translation."

"Oh, I have the New Living Translation," she said. "I'll use that."

"Great!" said the pastor, "See you tomorrow at church, God willing."

But Louella forgot one thing. She couldn't remember what time the service began, and she was a little embarrassed to ask the pastor. How could she have forgotten the schedule? Perhaps if she attended church regularly, service times would remain etched in her mind. At any rate, she was honored to have her pastor's confidence to read the Scripture. She would be ready.

As she crawled out of bed, she peeked at her backyard. The sun's rays cast a beautiful hue on her St. Augustine lawn. The glassy look of the dew on the grass brightened her mood, and the sound of birds singing outside gave her the impression that she would have a beautiful Saturday.

With confident strides that reflected her gratitude, she found her way into the bathroom. She was thankful to be alive. She was thankful for her health, and she started making a mental list of all the things that triggered her sense of gratitude—her work, her home, her neighborhood. Then she remembered she had a mortgage to pay at the end of the month, which always seemed to come sooner than expected, but she was approaching her final mortgage payments. The dividends from her flower business supported her sufficiently to make additional payments and pay off her home early. Once again, she recollected her litany of things for which she was grateful.

She went through her morning routine with relative ease, not that doing so presented a problem to her; she was just happy she didn't have a bad hair day. In any case, she didn't have to worry too much about her hair. It was Saturday morning, for crying out loud. She didn't have to dress like she was going to a beauty pageant. She wanted to have a relaxed and lazy day today and not have to worry about work or people or church.

Then she remembered she had something to do for the church. She had to prepare herself to read the Scriptures. She walked to her bookshelf to look for her Bible. Finding her copy of the New Living Translation took surprisingly long. She thought she would spot it off the shelf on the spur of the moment. She looked at the first shelf from left to right but couldn't see it. She moved to the next shelf below but still couldn't see it. The third shelf didn't yield much fruit either, all the way to the lowest shelf.

"That's funny," she said, "I could almost take an oath I placed my New Living Translation Bible on this shelf."

She started again from the top. As she got to the second shelf, she finally saw it. It was sitting directly in front of her as if to ask, "Can you see me now?"

"There you go," she spoke to her Bible. "So, you thought you were hiding. I found you, didn't I?" She picked it up as she would have picked up a pet, tucked it under her arm, and went to her recliner. She found the text of Scripture Pastor Matthew had given her, and she started reading it. She read it through several times, out loud, softly, by heart, and then out loud. She was sure she would nail it.

The day went by rather fast. She had several household chores she needed to do. First it was her laundry, then breakfast, then setting her house in order followed by putting her clothes in the dryer. She wondered if she could make a quick run to her local store to buy more essentials. As she tried to come up with a mental list of what she needed, her cell phone rang. It was Sam, her previous day's date. Her pulse began to pound as she picked up the phone.

"Louella? How are you today?"

"Sam!" She exclaimed. "How nice of you to call. I'm doing well. Thank you for asking. How are you?"

"Well, I'm doing well. I had a wedding planning gig earlier today, and then came to exercise. I just stepped out of the gym. I did some weights and just completed my cardio. Might you be available for dinner tonight, possibly around 5 pm?"

Once again, Louella wondered if Sam was moving too fast. Indeed, she thought he was. But then again, she didn't believe she was hurting anyone by being with Sam, so she consented.

"Of course!" She said, and then asked, "Where do you want to go?"

"How about Bill's Barbecue?"

"Oh! I love their ribs," she said. "See you there then."

She hung up the phone and went back to her previous train of thought. Lunchtime was coming soon, and she needed to get the household essentials before she ran out of time. It was amazing how the hours flew past her each day, especially on a Saturday when she needed to relax a little more.

After fixing herself a sandwich, she drove off to a dollar mart in Rockville. It was a convenient stopping spot for her due to its proximity to her house, and its prices were reasonable. As she stepped out of her car, she thought she saw Sam walking into the same store.

What a coincidence, she thought to herself. *He wouldn't be stalking me. How would he even know I was coming here?* To be sure, Sam was neither stalking her nor aware she was in that store. Otherwise, he wouldn't appear to be walking and holding hands with the blonde woman beside him. They seemed to be having a grand time, as if flirting and playing hide-and-seek among the store shelves. Louella's heart sank.

5

SATURDAY AFTERNOON SEEMED IDEAL to be at Rockville's Blue-Garden's Golf Club. It seemed every gentleman went there, either to hang out with friends or to play some golf. Some of them took it seriously while others cared very little how they fared provided they enjoyed themselves. Among them was James Dupree.

Dupree was a highly successful silver-haired businessman. He seemed to own a piece of property at just about every intersection in Rockville. His business, Dupree Enterprises, was a major source of income for Rockville residents. He had an inner circle of friends—people who helped him run his business. Some were members of his Board of Trustees; others were departmental directors; while still others were his advisors. Some were men and women who grew up in Rockville; others had relocated there either from out of state or from nearby Lockridge.

Rumor had it that Dupree might have employed some undocumented migrants in his enterprise though no one outside his inner circle of friends was entirely sure. Just the same, many jobseekers found his company instrumental in helping them put food on the table.

One thing, however, that only a few of his friends knew about Dupree was the fact that he was a go-getter. If he wanted something, nothing seemed to stop him from acquiring it. If he wanted someone hired, he would dig into his basket of persuasion techniques to convince his audience that such a person was best served working at Dupree Enterprises than anywhere else.

For whatever reason, Dupree heard about the flourishing flower shop in downtown Rockville at the corner of Main Street and Vine. Perhaps it was because this flower shop was the only supplier of wreaths and bouquets for funerals and weddings in this area. Many individuals had tried their hands at this business but failed. The proprietor of the flower shop was a gifted florist and certainly an erudite businessperson. Both were qualities Dupree admired. He longed to set up a booming business in this part of town, and no spot seemed more convenient than the flower shop and no person seemed more fitting for the job than Louella, its proprietor.

Unknown to Louella, Dupree had made an incognito visit to this shop. He had even purchased flowers for one of his company's staff recognition parties several weeks before. He was impressed with the efficiency with which Louella handled the orders he placed—precise, timely, and spot-on. If Louella joined his company as one of his staff members, he could go places with this business and with this partner!

Dupree completed his round of golf that afternoon and sat down with his buddies. The topics of discussion ranged from sports, entertainment, to serious business matters. Presently, he couldn't resist bringing up the topic of the downtown flower shop.

"You really seem surprisingly interested in that flower shop, Dupree," Mason Kruger, one of his trusted associates and legal counsel, remarked. "Why?"

"I just admire the way that lady runs that business," he said. "I wish I could buy that business, turn it into one of my franchises, and then employ her full-time. Do you know her name?"

"I think it's Loui,. . . Lou,. . . er, Louella. Yes! Louella," Mason recalled.

"Is there any chance we could set up a meeting with her and make a proposal?" Dupree asked.

"I don't see why not," said Mason. "We could always reach out to her informally and strike some kind of friendship, and then, once we feel comfortable bringing up the topic, we can make the suggestion."

"But we have to do it tactfully," Dupree said. "We don't want to make a proposal that would be dead on arrival."

"Of course not! We will be careful with it," Mason said.

They began formulating a strategy. It was the usual verbal and sketchy sort of brainstorming at first. But Dupree always liked to put things down on paper. In this way, any idea, however insignificant, would not be lost. He whipped out his notebook and began working on a plan of action as he listened to his associates offering various proposals.

Meanwhile, Louella was still standing at the dollar store quite aghast at the thought of seeing Sam flirting, or so she thought, with this girl who seemed ten years younger than he was. She walked over to Sam and made sure she established eye contact with him.

When Sam saw Louella, he blushed a little, but put on a brave face and said, "Oh! Hi Louella! I didn't think I would see you here. What brings you to the store?"

Louella could not believe Sam would ask her that question as if flirting with a girl this young was okay. But she remembered that she and Sam were not dating. No commitments had been made about their relationship with each other, so she decided to play along.

"I came to buy household items, essential household items. Who's this?" she asked about the woman.

"Louella, meet Nancy. Nancy is one of the clients at the gym that I've been training."

Louella was not sure what to say to Nancy, but she knew exactly what she needed to tell Sam.

"Well, about dinner tonight, maybe it's not a good idea," she said.

"Why, Louella? I thought we agreed to meet at 5 pm?" Sam seemed to protest.

What a player! He's flirting with a girl right before my eyes and then he asks me out right in this girl's hearing! He has no sense of decency. The day before she was getting very excited about finding someone she thought would be the one, and now she realized it was a pipe dream.

"Louella," Sam went on, "What you think you're seeing between Nancy and me is not what it is."

"I will talk to you later," Nancy told Sam. "I guess I have to go." Then turning to Louella, Nancy said, "I'm sorry about this. Good day to you both."

Sam looked confused. He neither expected Louella to show up nor anticipated Nancy to walk away. Louella gave him a serves-you-right kind of look, walked away to pick up the groceries she came for, paid for them, and headed for her car. She was breathing heavily, wondering how she almost got duped so easily.

Louella didn't know how she got home. She didn't remember driving through the stop lights and how she exited the highway into her neighborhood. She was too deep into her thoughts to realize she had reached home before she stepped hard on her brakes to avoid parking her car in her living room. She got out of her car, hurriedly picked up her stuff, fumbled with the keys to her house, dropping one item here and there and stooping to pick each one up. She couldn't believe she was reacting this way to what seemed like a failed date. She finally stepped into the house, laid everything on the kitchen table, walked into the living room, and plopped herself resignedly onto the couch. This was not how she'd hoped the day would end.

Louella sat on her couch until sunset. Given the way things turned out for her, she was quite content with having hot chocolate for dinner. Then she remembered she had an assignment from Pastor Matthew. The thought of reading Scripture on Sunday at church, with everything that had just happened, was not exciting to her. She wished someone else would read that passage. By 8 pm, she was ready to retire for the night. Not sure exactly whether she would sleep, she cleaned up, got into her pajamas, and curled herself into bed. It had been a day of mixed emotions.

6

Sunday morning was mostly quiet for Rockville residents. Traffic wasn't heavy, except on routes leading to different megachurches where Louella lived, and those were the exceptions rather than the rule. Louella preferred going to a smaller church where she had a better chance of knowing everybody compared to attending a larger church where she felt lost in the crowd. Besides, Pastor Matthew was a good preacher. His sermons were memorable and repeatable, easy for the attentive listener to follow.

Something, however, dampened her mood on this otherwise bright and beautiful Sunday morning: the previous day's experience with Sam. Immediately her countenance changed. She wasn't even sure she wanted to head out to church, let alone do the Bible reading as Pastor Matthew had requested. She picked up the phone to let him know she wouldn't be available to read on that day, but then she remembered she was asked to read because that day's reader was not feeling well. A last-minute cancelation would seriously inconvenience Pastor Matthew, so she got up and began getting ready for church.

After a quick shower, she dried herself, put on makeup, worked on her hair, chose the most appropriate outfit for a commanding stage presence, and slipped it on. She then went into the kitchen and fixed herself a quick breakfast, returned to the bathroom, brushed her teeth, and gave herself one last look in the mirror. Everything seemed fine. She wished her emotions were as confident as she looked, but who would know? She headed out the door, jumped into her car, and headed for church. As she would have expected, the only traffic she encountered was at the intersection by the megachurch near her home. She found it ironic that she had to drive by this huge church to find a smaller community of worship appropriate for her spiritual needs.

There it was, Rockville Community Church. A few cars were already at the parking lot. The Joneses, except Jeremy, were already there with their little one, probably about five years old. Mr. Smith and his wife, Julie, were also there. He always helped in leading the program. Louella couldn't remember failing to see Mr. Smith at the pulpit leading the call to worship or congregational singing every Sunday. He was always there, and quite a fixture he was. As she found a convenient spot to park her car, she stepped out and walked, somewhat shyly, toward the sanctuary. Pastor Matthew was already at the door having a chat with some of the early arrivals.

"Well, who do we have here?" he said. "Welcome to the service, Louella. Am I glad to see you. Thank you very much for taking up the reading on such a short notice."

"I'm glad you asked me, Pastor," Louella responded. "I hope it goes well!"

"Listen," Pastor Matthew said, "how about you, Mr. Smith, and I go back into my office and have a quick program run-through? In this way we'll all be on the same page about how the program plays itself out during the service."

"Fine with me," said Louella as she followed Pastor Matthew into his office.

Mr. Smith was right behind them. They exchanged pleasantries and chatted briefly about politics and the county's recent events, including the half-marathon that took place the previous day. The conversation quickly evolved into the program for that day, and Pastor Matthew went through the items in the bulletin, including the order of service, and they were ready for church. Both Pastor Matthew and Mr. Smith prayed and paused to see if Louella would pray. She had never been confident praying out loud in public before, and she wasn't sure she would say the right words.

"Lord," she said, "we thank you for giving us this opportunity to worship you. Please watch over the service, and over our pastor as he brings the sermon. In your name we pray, Amen."

"Amen," they all repeated, as if on cue.

The service started with familiar hymns, hymns Louella grew up singing not just in Sunday school but also in different worship contexts. Her time came to read the Scripture, and with a quivering voice, she started off with the first sentence from the text. The sound of her voice coming through the speaker startled her. She gained some confidence, and by the time she was through with the reading, she had forgotten about her fears.

The pastor's sermon really touched her heart. She couldn't remember everything Pastor Matthew said, but she did remember the theme and main points of the sermon: "Bring your problems to Jesus because (1) no problem is too small for his attention, (2) no problem is too sizeable for his ability, and (3) no problem is too stubborn for his authority." Louella was impressed that Pastor Matthew was able to extract such a powerful and meaningful sermon from the text in Mark 1:29–34. She absolutely loved it.

Since she was seated up front with Mr. Smith and the pastor, she looked around at members of the congregation to see if they, too, were as captivated by the sermon as she was. Everyone seemed to hang on the pastor's every word. It was powerful. It was eloquent. It seemed to come from the throne of God himself. The 300-seat capacity sanctuary was almost full. She then noticed a face she had seen before at her flower shop. She wasn't sure about that face, but she could almost swear that the silver-haired, middle-aged gentleman seated almost at the last pew had stopped by her business premises the previous Friday. She looked closely and noticed another familiar face—Sam!

Sam goes to this church? She wondered about this and was embarrassed that her thoughts were almost loud enough to be heard. She didn't even get the impression that Sam was a Christian though she did remember hearing him say he was on his own pilgrimage and that he was not a regular churchgoer but did attend service from time to time. Moreover, he seemed to be sitting next to the silver-haired gentleman. Perhaps it was mere coincidence. Perhaps they knew each other. Perhaps this was someone that looked like Sam. Her thoughts raced wildly. Oh, Sam! Why does she even bother thinking about him when he seemed to let her down the way he did the day before? As she was thinking about Sam, her thoughts were interrupted by Pastor Matthew's closing words and the invitation to sing the final hymn.

The service was over. She headed for the door and noticed Sam standing outside, directly on her path toward her car. He extended his hand to greet her. She wasn't sure she could do it. But she extended hers anyway.

"Hi Louella," said Sam, "What a nice reading voice you have!'

"Thank you, Sam," she said, and then exclaimed, "I didn't know you go to church!"

"I do sometimes," he said. "I've been coming here for the past couple of weeks but only intermittently. I kind of like it. Pastor Matthew is a really good preacher."

"I thought you didn't care much about spiritual things," Louella seemed to recall from their first conversation.

"I'm searching just like everybody else," Sam said. "Listen," he went on, "about yesterday, I'm really sorry. I didn't mean to come across to you the way I did with Nancy."

"Don't sweat it," Louella said. "If you have someone in your life, I don't really mind. What I do mind is the fact that you didn't tell me this up front. I did ask you if you had someone in your life, and you gave me a negative answer, so either you hooked up with Nancy in less than 24 hours before you asked me out on a date, or you weren't telling me the truth."

"Hello," a silver-haired, middle-aged gentleman extended his hand toward Louella, interrupting her well-choreographed speech. "My name is James Dupree. May I please shake your hand?"

7

Somewhat taken aback by the greeting, Louella muttered something back, almost as if she blurted out two words simultaneously. Then she regained her composure and shook Mr. Dupree's hand.

"Hello, Sir," she said.

"You read very well," Mr. Dupree went on. "I also happen to know you though I suspect you don't know me."

"You do look familiar," Louella replied, "and I think I've seen you at my flower shop although it is possible I'm confusing you with someone else. People tend to look alike, you know."

"Yes, I did stop by your shop, and I have to say I'm truly impressed by your work ethic and by your ability to sustain that business single-handedly. Would you care to share with me how you began?"

Louella was not sure she needed to give Mr. Dupree all the pieces of information he was looking for. She was talking to Mr. Dupree for the very first time, and it seemed to her she would be giving away valuable information to a person she hardly knew.

"I don't believe I have the time to share the history of my flower shop with you," she told him. "Perhaps I could do it on another day."

"How about we all meet at the Town House Coffee tomorrow after work, possibly at 6:00 pm, and then we can get to hear your story?" Sam offered.

Louella couldn't believe her ears. Sam was asking her out on a date again?

"Now, why would I do that?" Louella asked.

"Louella, I do know Mr. Dupree," Sam said. "And you need not be hesitant to meet with him and me just to hear your story. Nancy, the girl you found me talking with at the grocery store, is Mr. Dupree's daughter, and Mr. Dupree and my dad are distant cousins."

"What?" Louella asked. "You mean to tell me you and Nancy are blood related? Why didn't you tell me that before?"

"Well, every time I tried to tell you about it, you cut me off," Sam said. "I'm not seeing anyone in my life at this point. Nancy is a blood relative and, of course, I'm not seeing her. She just looks up to me as her big brother!"

It was time for Louella to feel embarrassed. She realized she had jumped to conclusions too quickly.

"I'm *so* sorry for being *so* judgmental," she said. "I'm also sorry for canceling the dinner on you yesterday."

"Well, you have an opportunity to make it right," Sam said. "I would probably have done the same thing if I was in your shoes. So, are we good? Can we meet tomorrow with Mr. Dupree?"

"I guess it would be perfectly alright," Louella answered.

Turning to Mr. Dupree, she said, "Please convey my apologies to your daughter. I didn't mean to be so rude and offensive. It's just that I got really miffed when I erroneously assumed Sam was flirting with your daughter."

"Nancy looks up to Sam just as if Sam was her elder brother," Dupree said, "And I would be honored to express your sentiments to her. So, I hope I get to see you tomorrow."

They parted ways. Sam and Mr. Dupree walked toward a black Jeep Wagoneer parked under the shade of the oak tree almost at the heart of the parking lot. They both jumped in and left. Louella kept standing at the same spot, observing them drive off onto the main highway.

"Louella, you sounded great," came the voice of Pastor Matthew from behind her as the door of the church closed. Pastor Matthew was shutting down the building to head home. His wife, Sharon, and two precious boys were right next to him, having spent time talking with other members of the congregation.

"Thank you very much, Pastor! I was truly honored to do it. By the way," Louella went on, "that was an excellent sermon you gave us this morning. I'm glad I got to read the text for today but also to hear what the Lord had in store for us."

After saying their goodbyes to each other, Louella walked to her car, jumped in, and drove off. As she headed home, she rebuked herself for not giving Sam the benefit of the doubt concerning Nancy. On the one hand, she was happy Sam was, after all, not cheating on her, even though they weren't seeing each other. On the other hand, she was embarrassed by her outburst because it betrayed her assumption about wanting to be in a relationship with Sam. She didn't want Sam to know that she was thinking of him in those terms. Her outburst gave her away. Monday 5 pm would be an interesting unfolding of the evening for both.

Her thoughts were interrupted by her cell phone ringing. It came from a certain gentleman named Mason. Mason was one of Dupree's right-hand men. He was calling to confirm the meeting with Mr. Dupree.

"Is this Louella?" he asked.

"This is she," she replied.

"I understand you had a conversation with Mr. Dupree about meeting tomorrow, and I'm just calling to confirm this so I can put it in my calendar."

Louella found it strange at the official turn the dinner meeting had taken. This was supposed to be an informal dinner gathering to tell her story about her flower shop. It wasn't supposed to be a job interview. At any rate, she decided to go with the flow.

"Yes, we do have a meeting over dinner," she said, as if to tell Mason directly that it was not as official as he was trying to make it out to be. She then went on, "I'll be sharing my story with him and Sam about the birth and growth of my flower business."

"Oh! That's wonderful," Mason said. "I look forward to hearing that story myself. See you tomorrow!"

"Wait a minute," Louella said, quite surprised. "Are you also planning on being there? This meeting is between Mr. Dupree, Sam, and me."

"You can be sure that if I know of a meeting, like I now do, Mr. Dupree wants me to be there," Mason said. "But don't be alarmed," he went on, "because I'll be there merely to ascertain the fact that such a meeting did indeed take place."

"Okay," said Louella. "I guess I'll get to see you tomorrow then. Have a blessed day." Louella hung up the phone. She felt somewhat uneasy about the meeting with one more person added in. She wasn't sure, at this rate, if the maximum number of attendees at the meeting would remain at three. Perhaps she'll be speaking to a crowd of people.

Upon arriving home, she walked into the kitchen and fixed herself a sandwich. She wasn't as sad on Sunday as she had been the previous day. Sam had cleared the air for her. She didn't have to worry about Nancy flirting with Sam, and she was looking forward to spending the rest of the day indoors.

8

MONDAY WAS ALWAYS A slow day for Louella. One couldn't blame her for that. Everyone seemed immobilized by the previous weekend's excitement, stemming from partying, taking children to soccer matches and baseball games, or simply watching movies all day. For people of faith like Louella, church activities did make her tired though feeling tired from reading Scripture on Sunday was hardly a good explanation for the slow start to the day.

Customers walked in and out of her flower shop intermittently. Some greeted her verbally; others merely nodded. Many more simply walked in, found what they wanted, checked out, and made a bolt for the door as if chasing something urgent. Louella simply watched the customers from her seat, now responding to questions for directions, now specifying the unposted price of a bouquet of flowers.

The day went by rather quickly, probably much faster than she really wished for it to go. She was dreading her meeting with Mr. Dupree, especially after receiving the unexpected phone call from Mason, Dupree's apparent right-hand man. She calmed her nerves by assuring herself that she was only sharing the history of her business and nothing more. Besides, it was her story; it belonged to her. She didn't need to modify it or change it in any way. She didn't see the big deal behind this fact. Just the same, she remained nervous.

Before she knew it, the clock struck five. As she started shutting down her premises, her cell phone rang, and she answered it.

"Louella?" came a voice from the other end of the line.

"This is she," she responded. "How can I help you?"

"This is Mr. Dupree, just confirming that we are meeting tonight at 6."

"Yes, we are," she replied. "I'm just shutting down the shop, and I'll be on the road to . . . where was that again?"

"Townhouse Coffee House," Mr. Dupree clarified.

"Ah! Yes," she said, "I know where that is. Right by Jones Bank."

"Exactly," Mr. Dupree said, "I'm heading over there right now. See you soon." He then hung up the phone.

Louella wondered how Mr. Dupree got her number. *Sam*, she thought. *Sam must have given him my number without my consent.*

Immediately she called Sam who seemed to be waiting for her call because it barely rang before she heard Sam's now familiar voice at the end of the line.

"Hi, Louella," he said, "So nice of you to call."

"Hi, Sam," she replied, and went on, "Did you happen to give Mr. Dupree my number?"

Sam sounded genuinely shocked and defensive in his tone, "My goodness! No!" he said. "I'm more professional than that. Why do you ask?"

"Well," she replied, "He called me a moment ago, and I don't remember giving him my number." Then she remembered how Mason called her the previous day, and she couldn't think how he, too, got her number. She went on, "And now that I think about it, Mason also called me yesterday. I've never met him before, and he called me on this number. How did these two people know my number?"

"I can assure you," Sam went on, "that I neither gave Mason nor Mr. Dupree your number. Remember, though, that you do have a business card on your counter at the shop. That's how I got your number because I knew I'd need to call you about placing orders for flowers. Might these two gentlemen have gained access to your number that way?"

That explanation made perfect sense to Louella. "That's a very reasonable explanation," she said, and added, "Well, I'm closing the flower shop for the day and will be making my way to Town House Coffee. See you there."

"Okay. See you soon!" Sam responded, but with a sigh of relief. Indeed, he had passed on Louella's number to Dupree, but he also remembered seeing Louella's business card in her flower shop sitting by the business counter. That's how he got Louella's number. Louella's name was on it, and her business, Rockville's Finest Flowers, LLC, was printed next to a flowery logo depicting different colors of flowers in a vase. Because things had gone sour between him and Louella three days before, he wasn't prepared for any verbal altercations with Louella if he could avoid it. He wanted to preserve the relationship and perhaps see it go further than where it had reached already.

Louella made it to the restaurant at 5:50 pm. Sam, Mason, and Mr. Dupree were already seated by a roundtable in what seemed to be a secluded corner to the left of the entrance. There was only one other seat left, and Louella figured they had left it for her. Mr. Dupree and Mason sat, roughly, on one side while Sam sat next to Louella as if they were setting her up for a date.

The waitress who had received her at the door invited her to sit, and the men at the table sounded excited to see her.

"Hi, Louella," Sam said. "It's good to see you!"

"Hi, Sam," she said and went on to greet Mason and Mr. Dupree. "Hi, Mason. Hi, Mr. Dupree." Responding in kind, their handshakes were firm. She wondered whether they found her handshake too weak, perhaps even betraying her reluctance at being at that meeting. It seemed more like an interview than it did a time out for dinner.

"It was good to see you yesterday," said Mr. Dupree. "And I am particularly excited to hear your story tonight. How did you begin and what is the secret of your success?"

"Can I get you all something to drink?" the waitress assigned to them interrupted. "What would you like to drink, Ma'am?" she asked, beginning with Louella.

"Can I get some strawberry lemonade, please? Please go easy on the ice," Louella answered. The waitress took down the order and then turned to the men. Mr. Dupree asked for iced tea while Sam got diet Coke and Mason settled for water.

"Okay. Great! I'll get these to you in a minute. Thank you!" The waitress left almost as immediately as she had arrived.

"Wonderful," Mason said.

"Now, where were we?" Mr. Dupree asked. "Yes! You were beginning to tell us the story of how you began your business."

"Yes, I was," replied Louella. "For the benefit of the two of you," she said, pointing to Mason and Mr. Dupree, "I'll share with you what I shared with Sam several days ago. I've been running this business for the past three years. I got a loan from my mortgage lender as starting capital, and it pretty much funded the setting up of the business. It has been running quite well, and I'm on course not only to pay off the loan but also to pay off my mortgage."

"That is remarkable," Mason observed. "Your work ethic is amazing."

"You see, Louella," said Mr. Dupree, "I have a business proposal for you. I'm in serious need of disciplined individuals such as yourself, and I wonder if you might be interested in a business partnership with Dupree Enterprises."

This gesture surprised Louella. "What kind of partnership do you have in mind?" she asked.

"What if we combine forces where we come as equal partners?" Mr. Dupree went on, "What if I pay off the remaining balance on your loan and then have you become an employee of my company, earning a salary twice the amount you earn from your business profits?"

Louella was flattered that somebody of Mr. Dupree's caliber was really interested in her abilities, and not only her abilities but also her business. Even more surprising to her was the fact that it came from Mr. Dupree, the most respected businessman in Rockville. The same voice that seemed to urge her to accept Sam's request for a date screamed in her head again. *Say, "Yes!" Say, "Yes!"* Another voice, perhaps more reasonable than the first one, warned her to proceed with caution, possibly even halt the advance and not make any decisions before giving it some serious thought.

Louella listened to the second voice. She remembered how she had struggled to set up the business and how she had worked hard to find a convenient spot in Rockville to locate the business. If she handed all that hard-earned achievement to Mr. Dupree, who didn't even give her a good reason for wanting to buy her business, her legacy would be destroyed.

"Thank you for the proposal, Mr. Dupree," Louella said, "But let me give it some thought since your request is coming to me for the very first time. I want to be sure that whatever decision I make, it will be based on careful reflection on the pros and cons."

"You need not worry about that," Mason said. "We have looked at possible scenarios and outcomes of this business venture, and we think you'll be pleased with what we're offering you. Whatever profits you're earning from your business, we'll double, and you will be one of the CEOs in your partnership with Mr. Dupree."

"Again," said Louella, "please give me time to think about this. I could decline your offer right now and continue to do what I'm doing, which, by the way, I enjoy doing immensely. But I'm also giving you the benefit of the doubt by asking you to allow me to think about it. I want to know what legal implications follow such decisions, and I need to be in touch with a good lawyer to help me think about this."

"You need not worry about finding a lawyer," Mason continued. "I'm Mr. Dupree's lawyer, and I help him with counsel on such matters, from start to finish. You'll not even need to pay the legal fees. They'll be waived by virtue of what we're trying to accomplish today. However, out of respect for your request, we will certainly give you time to think about this offer."

"Thank you," said Louella. "I really appreciate your flexibility on this issue."

"You need to bear in mind, Louella," Sam interrupted, "that Mr. Dupree is a very successful businessman. I think you'll enjoy working with him in this partnership."

While they were still speaking, the waitress brought their drinks, placed them on the table, and then took their meal orders. Throughout the evening, Mr. Dupree kept painting a fantastic picture of what his partnership with Louella would look like and what they could achieve financially. Louella merely listened. The more Mr. Dupree talked, the more Louella felt persuaded to accept the proposal.

The waitress returned with their orders. As the men chomped away, Louella chewed reflectively. She needed time to think and could hardly bring herself to the present though she smiled approvingly at the humor the men were throwing at each other with every sentence. Sam was particularly wordy, possibly trying to win himself back into Louella's good graces, but also being careful not to seem too dramatic and excessive. They finished their meals and began talking about heading back to their homes.

"When do you think we will hear from you?" Mr. Dupree asked Louella.

"Give me about five days. I think I might come back to you with an answer on Friday," Louella responded.

Mr. Dupree wanted to press her for an earlier date, but Mason interrupted, saying, "Friday is good enough! So, what shall we say, come back here on Friday, maybe?"

"Of course," Louella said. "But this is contingent upon the fact that I will have made my decision by then. If not, please give me more time to think about it. Either way, I will let you know."

"You need to realize, Louella," Mr. Dupree said, almost in a patronizing way, "that this is going to be something really big for you, for us, for this town. We would want you to decide as soon as possible."

"Okay," Louella said. "But do give me time to think about it."

They said their goodbyes. Sam walked to his truck, which he drove the first time he and Louella met at Town House Coffee. Mason and Mr. Dupree walked toward the Jeep Wagoneer, which Louella had seen the day before at the community church. Their cars started almost simultaneously and soon headed out the parking lot onto the highway. Louella walked toward her car and drove home, once again, exhausted, thoughtful, and somewhat confused.

9

When Louella walked into her house, she went straight to her bedroom and began to prepare for bed. But before she could sleep, she knew she had an important decision to make. Would she really give up three years of establishing a legacy in Rockville to become the CEO of one of the leading businesses in Rockville? She wasn't sure about the terms of engagement and whether she would be an equal partner with Mr. Dupree. She wasn't even sure how Sam fitted into this picture. The more she thought about this, the more confused she became. She was in desperate need of wisdom and counsel.

At that point she remembered what the pastor had preached about the previous Sunday: Bring your problems to Jesus because (1) no problem is too small for his attention, (2) no problem is too sizeable for his ability,and (3) no problem is too stubborn for his authority. She had read the Scripture on which Pastor Matthew's outline was based. She knew she needed help with counsel . . . desperately.

So Louella found herself going down on her knees by her bedside and prayed, "Dear Lord Jesus Christ, based on the sermon your servant preached to us yesterday and on the Scriptures from which he preached that powerful sermon, I now ask you to show me the way. Give me guidance on how to respond to Mr. Dupree. Should I accept the offer, or should I turn it down? Most importantly, give me peace about the answer I will give Mr. Dupree." Louella had never prayed like this before. Most of the time things seemed to work on their own without her needing to pray. But on this day, she believed she needed divine help. Surprisingly, a sense of peace enveloped her entire being. She found herself strangely at ease, a sharp contrast compared to how she felt while at Town House Coffee.

Once she got ready for bed, she lay down and turned on her bedroom TV. A famous late night talk show aired on one of the channels. She found herself dozing off and getting startled repeatedly, so she turned off her TV and her bedside lights. Something about the conversation at Town House Coffee replayed itself in her mind repeatedly. Mr. Dupree's messiah complex, Mason's self-confidence, and Sam's loudness kept haunting her simultaneously. The short bedside prayer, however, assured her that all was in God's hands. Tomorrow was another day, and she needed to be well rested before she ventured out to her flower shop. Before she knew it, she was sound asleep.

Tuesday morning came sooner than Louella really wanted, but she was excited to head out to her shop. For some reason, traffic into her shop was quite heavy compared to the previous day. Money was coming in quite fast. Business had not been this good for the larger part of the month. The checkout line was long. She knew she needed an assistant, but this wasn't the time to begin worrying about it. She had work to do, and she did it.

Occasionally, she would stop attending to a customer at the checkout counter in order to attend to another customer at the aisles needing pieces of advice on what flowers to buy for what occasion. These interruptions slowed down the process and elevated the frustration of some customers. Perhaps, she thought, it would be a good idea, after all, to hand this business over to Mr. Dupree. In this way she wouldn't have to deal with the frustrations she was facing. Still, she knew she loved her work.

By the time she closed her shop that day, she had made more money than she made the previous week. The business on that day was almost as profitable as what she earned on Valentine's Day. Louella scratched her head trying to understand what accounted for that day's success. She still couldn't explain it. At any rate, she accepted the fact that it was one of her most successful days, and she was thankful for it.

Then she remembered she still had a decision to make before Friday. That fact somewhat dampened her spirits. Did she really want to walk away from her livelihood to become a CEO? Did she really want to join ranks, at such a significantly high level, with someone she had met or seen only three times before? She remained uncertain about this fact. For now, however, she celebrated her success as she drove home. Perhaps this was an indication that she didn't have to close shop for good after all.

In the meantime, Mr. Dupree was surprised that Louella had not called him to accept the offer. He thought doubling her earnings on any given day or month would be attractive terms of engagement for such an offer.

"Mason," Mr. Dupree asked, "Have you heard from Louella yet?"

Mason was sitting in the adjacent office, but his door was open, and he could hear Mr. Dupree's question coming from his office. "No sir," said Mason. "I haven't heard from her at all."

"I'm giving her a very generous offer, one many people would kill to have," Mr. Dupree said, "She would be absolutely foolish not to take it."

"I know," Mason said. "But let's give her until Friday."

"I don't want to wait until Friday!" bellowed Mr. Dupree. "I want that business location, and I want it now for my other projects!"

"You'll get that location," said Mason. "But you've got to have patience. These things take time."

Mr. Dupree always stopped at nothing to get whatever he wanted. It infuriated him that Louella effectively hindered his bulldozing personality. Afterall, he was the most successful businessman in Rockville. He thought that fact alone should have given him an immediate affirmative nod from Louella.

"Why not call her to see what direction she's leaning towards?" Mr. Dupree suggested. "I don't like wasting time."

"No, I'd rather not," Mason replied. "Give it some time. In the meantime, I'll be drafting some terms for the contract so that if she says "Yes," the contract will be already in place."

"If?" asked Mr. Dupree. "You mean to say you are doubtful she will accept this offer? No one ever turns me down. Absolutely no one."

"I understand," said Mason.

But before Mason could say anything else, Mr. Dupree interrupted him, "You understand nothing! No one turns me down! Absolutely no one!"

"I understand," said Mason again, which agitated Mr. Dupree even more, causing him to bang his desk in the other room.

"Sorry! You're right! I don't understand," Mason sheepishly responded. "So what do you suggest I do?" he asked.

"Call her!" bellowed Mr. Dupree. "Let her know I'm waiting for an answer and that answer had better be in the affirmative!"

"But sir . . ."

"No buts!" Mr. Dupree interrupted. "I can't be held hostage by a woman who started her business only three years ago and is now preparing to dominate the business world with her flower shop. No one outbids me in this industry!"

"Okay, sir!" Mason yielded. "I'll call her right away."

The phone startled Louella as she drove home. She saw Mason's name on the caller ID.

This is unbelievable, she thought. *What would he be calling me for at this time?* She then picked up the phone and said, "Hello!"

"Hello, Louella," Mason responded. "How are you today?"

"I'm well," Louella replied.

"I was just calling to check on you and see how you're doing," Mason said.

"How kind of you!" Louella responded, more as a matter of politeness than of telling the truth.

"I was also calling," Mason continued, "to find out if you might have given any further thought to the discussion we had yesterday."

These guys are unrelenting, Louella thought. "I'm still thinking about it," Louella answered. "When I reach my decision, I'll let you know," she continued.

"Please know that we would be delighted to have you on board in our organization." Mason went on. "We could use people with your kind of skills."

"I'm thankful that you think so highly of me." Louella answered. "But please give me time to think about all these. It's a big decision for me, and I can't jump into it without knowing what I'm getting into."

"Oh! I can help you with that," said Mason. "I've already drafted the terms of engagement should you decide to join us. Would you like to see the document?"

"Sure," Louella said, believing it wouldn't hurt for her to know what she was getting herself into. The more information she had at her fingertips, the better. "Please send it along."

"Fantastic!" said Mason. "Kindly text me your email address and I'll send you a copy!"

"You got it!" Louella said and hung up. She finally pulled into her driveway, stopped the engine, and walked into the house. Before she could do anything else, she texted her email address to Mason and started preparing her dinner. A home-cooked meal seemed more attractive that evening than eating out. As she prepared her food, she heard her phone beep. *I think that's Mason, possibly acknowledging my text*, she thought. She walked over to her phone and checked the message. She was right. Mason acknowledged the arrival of her text. She only needed to wait for the document detailing the terms of engagement.

As she fixed her dinner, she wondered if those terms included items that needed additional interpretation, none of which she thought she was qualified to do. Perhaps she needed her own lawyer to help her know what hidden details might accompany that document. The more she thought about it, the more she found it necessary to get an extra set of eyes, a legal mind, to help confirm to her that what she was looking at was what she would get. She was fearful of falling victim to fraud, and she knew that Rockville had more than its fair share of fraudulent activity. As she went through these thoughts, her dinner was ready. It was nothing spectacular, just spaghetti and meatballs with parmesan cheese, salad, and a can of Sprite. She didn't think she needed an elaborate meal. For her, meals were tasty only when she had company. Once her meal was done, she cleaned up, brushed her teeth, and got ready for bed as she watched the late-night news. Her day had been an interesting one: successful businesswise but uncertain as far as her decision about Mr. Dupree's proposal was concerned. But she hit the pillow and, almost immediately, drifted off to sleep.

10

Louella woke up Wednesday morning with a determinate effort to read Mason's document in its entirety. After checking her email, she saw a new one in her inbox from Mason Kruger. *That must be the one*, she thought to herself. She opened it, and it seemed painfully long. It was a 16-page document. She sighed heavily. She wasn't sure she was in a position to read through all the details contained in the document. But she remembered her resolve as she woke up that morning, and she promised to find the time to read the document later that day.

Work was as usual though not as busy as the previous day. She knew she needed to hire more assistants to help when customer traffic was heavy, so she decided to post a "Now Hiring" sign outside her door. She went to her computer, typed out the sign and printed the document on hard manilla paper. Though not entirely adept at computer graphics, she was pleased with the result. It would serve the purpose of what she was trying to accomplish.

She posted the sign on her door and waited to see if anyone would be interested in the advert. Those passing by stopped to read the details below the large print and then kept going. Some paused to take the telephone number she had posted. *It looked promising*, she thought. Then she remembered, *what if she chooses to take the offer from Mr. Dupree? What will become of her new hire?* This prompted her to open the document Mason sent her. She started looking through it. It was full of legal jargon, some of which she had to read several times to understand its contents or even get the general trajectory of its meaning. The more she read it, however, the more confused she got. When she completed reading the document, she wasn't sure what the contract entailed. If she was leaning towards the possibility of taking the job, the uncertainty created by the document led her into the opposite direction. She wasn't going to sign up for something whose terms remained unclear to her. Since not too many customers were coming into her shop, she decided to call Mason.

"Hello," Mason's voice could be heard at the other end of the line.

"Mason? Hi. This is Louella," she said.

"Hi Louella!" he replied. "How are you doing today?"

"I'm well, thank you," was her reply. "I wanted to speak to you about the document you sent me."

"Okay. Have you read it?" Mason asked.

"Yes, I have," she said. "I just finished reading it. But I can tell you that I understood very little of all that stuff you wrote in there. I'm not ready to sign a contract whose terms I don't understand."

"Well, I can help explain everything to you," Mason said. "If you have a minute, I can do that."

"Go on," she said.

"I can give you the bullet points of what the contract entails. Mr. Dupree's company will buy your business and will also pay off the loan you took out to underwrite the cost of establishing the business, as well as pay off your mortgage. In addition, Mr. Dupree's company will pay you a salary twice the amount of the average annual profit brought in by your business. I think that's a great plan. Don't you think?"

"Hearing it from you," Louella replied, "It sounds nice and rosy. What I don't understand is how what you've said corresponds to what's on paper. Moreover, the language trying to capture my additional benefits is way beyond my understanding. Listen, I was and I'm still happy with where I am with my business. Why don't you find someone else that fits your business plan and hire that person? I don't need to join you in your business goals. They seem quite different from mine."

"Listen," Mason insisted, "Why don't you, Mr. Dupree, and I sit down again to clarify the details hammered out in this contract? I think a face-to-face meeting will help us all out."

Louella wasn't ready to have another meeting with either of them. She was sure very little would be accomplished in that meeting. She knew she was leaning toward declining the offer. Perhaps this was God's way of telling her to walk away. God? Why had she not thought of him since she prayed on Monday night? Could it be that he was beginning to reveal to her what she didn't know previously? If this was his way of speaking to her, it was happening loud and clear. Her heart skipped a beat. She had placed her need before God in prayer, and two days later, God was giving her an answer. She felt quite at peace with that decision; the same peace had engulfed her immediately after she prayed for guidance beside her bed.

"Let me save you and Mr. Dupree the effort and time you want to spend meeting with me," Louella said. "I'm more than confident I don't wish to pursue this matter with you. But thank you for considering me for the position of CEO in your company." She said this and hung up.

Mason wasn't ready for her answer as the disengaged phone beeped in his ear. He pulled it off his ear and looked at the phone, as if the phone itself had turned him down. As he hoisted his hand to smash it on the floor, it rang. He could tell from the caller ID that Mr. Dupree was trying to reach him. Mason was in the office; Mr. Dupree was out in the field, inspecting his other business franchises.

"Yes, sir," Mason said as he picked up Mr. Dupree's call.

"Well?" Mr. Dupree started, "Do you have any updates for me?"

"I do, sir," Mason said, "And it's not good news. Louella has turned down the offer."

"Mason!" Mr. Dupree responded, half shouting and half screaming out his name. "No one ever turns me down. Since she's gone this direction, you know what we do in these kinds of situations, don't you?"

"Yes sir," Mason replied.

"Don't you?!" Mr. Dupree asked again, with greater emphasis.

"Yes, sir! I do," Mason replied.

"Well, get to work then. Make sure that business is incapacitated by morning!"

Although Mason knew what Mr. Dupree wanted him to do, he was reluctant to do it. They had acquired many businesses in this way, rendering their owners financially impotent. He wasn't sure he wanted Louella to be their latest victim. *Why can't Mr. Dupree be original enough to start his own business without arm-twisting entrepreneurs into surrendering their hard-earned legacies to him?* he wondered.

Meanwhile, Louella felt a deep sense of satisfaction about the decision she'd made. She carried on with her work, feeling triumphant about the day's unfolding of events. A few more customers walked in to make purchases, and she served them gleefully. As she approached her closing hours, the phone rang. Someone was inquiring about the hiring advert posted on her door. She explained the nature of the job in detail. She simply needed an assistant. Someone to help the customers find what they were looking for as she worked by the checkout counter. She set up an interview with the caller for Thursday, 9:00 am. Louella was ecstatic. Her business, at last, had the potential of growing by at least one person!

She shut down the shop at 5 pm and headed home. As she remained optimistic about the successful business transactions she'd had the previous day and how she turned down the offer from Mr. Dupree, she traveled home with a sense of triumph. She was beginning to appreciate her own autonomy and independence. Her home routine was as before: dinner—cleanup—TV—bed. While in bed, she began dozing off, so she turned off the TV, turned onto her right side, faced the wall, and drifted off to sleep.

11

LOUELLA'S SLEEP WAS RUDELY interrupted by her doorbell ringing. She looked at the clock. It was 3:39 am, Thursday. Louella wasn't sure what to make of it. She looked at her security camera to see who was at her doorstep. It was a police officer. *That's strange,* she thought, *why would a police officer be knocking at my door at this hour*? She walked to the door and opened it.

"Hello," said the police officer, "we are looking for Louella Goodman."

"That's me," said Louella, "What can I do for you?"

"You're the proprietor of Rockville's Finest Flowers, right?" The policeman asked.

"I'm the owner," She replied.

"I'm afraid to say your business has been vandalized and we need you to come and assess the damage."

Louella's heart sank. She wondered why anyone would want to vandalize her shop. It wasn't one of the most attractive business premises in town despite being located in a convenient spot for business. This wasn't the kind of news she wanted to hear. She quickly changed from her pajamas into her regular clothes, found her purse and keys, and jumped into her car. With hands trembling, she turned on the ignition key. It wouldn't start. She tried again. This time the engine cranked, choked, and started. *Why don't these things work properly when you need them most?* She wondered as she backed out of her driveway. The police officer was already ahead of her. Since it was early in the morning, there wasn't much traffic on the highway, so she merely kept up with the police officer's speed, who seemed to be going ten miles per hour above the speed limit.

They both arrived at Rockville's Finest Flowers. Several squad cars were at the scene with their lights flashing. They used "do-not-cross" tape to cordon off the business premises because it was an active crime scene.

The front door glass had been shattered. The door was open. Several flowers were lying carelessly on the floor. The cash register had been forcefully pulled back. All the money was gone. The flowers kept in the fridge were all strewn on the floor. Clearly, the intruder or intruders meant to do as much damage as they could. Louella pulled her hair in shock and horror.

"Who would do such a thing?" she asked no one in particular. She'd been given a pass into the cordoned off area to help the investigators assess the damage. The police officer led her into the building and introduced her to another plainclothes policeman. She wasn't looking up at the policeman at all. She was still shaken by what used to be a neatly arranged flower shop that was now unrecognizable from the mess.

The plainclothes detective raised his hand as if to beckon her forward. "Ma'am," he said, "please step over here." She looked up from all the mess strewn on the floor into the eyes of a slim smartly dressed detective. He went on, "Did you leave any money in the cash register, and, if so, how much?"

Luckily, she had taken all the days earnings home with her and planned to stop by the nearby bank in the morning to make a deposit.

Amid tears, Louella answered, "I had taken out all the money, and it's in my house right now. I was planning to take it to the bank this morning. Jesus! Who would do such a thing?"

The detective went on with his questioning, "Would you have any idea who might have done this?"

Louella answered, "I'm asking myself the same question. I don't know who could have done it!"

The detective who knocked at her door carried on with his own sets of questions: "Ma'am, we're trying the best we can to catch the thief. I see you have surveillance cameras in your premises here. Do they work?" Her eyes lit up. She'd forgotten about the cameras.

"Of course they do." She tried to log into her computer but, it, too, was smashed. Thankfully, her phone came in handy. She was able to log into her phone and open the surveillance camera app. She then became a front-seat audience to the crime. She saw it unfold as two masked men hurled two bricks into the building. The glass shattered inward from the force of the bricks. They walked in and began pulling the flowers off the shelves and out of the refrigerators. One jumped over the counter and smashed the cash register open with his crowbar. He seemed rather furious when he found no cash and swung his crowbar violently at the computer screen sitting above the cash register. Something seemed to startle them, however. It was the burglar alarm. Before they could do further damage, they took off, jumped into their Chevy Malibu, and drove off at top speed. The outside camera caught it on tape.

"You're very lucky to have had this app on your phone," said the detective. "We'll need a copy of that video to help with the investigations. Do you have insurance for your property?"

"As a matter of fact, I do. I have to wait until daybreak to file a claim," Louella said.

"You do know that most insurance companies have 24-hour service seven days a week," replied the detective. "I suggest you call them immediately and strike while the iron is still hot. In the meantime, allow us to file a police report. For now, though, you have no option but to shut down your business until we resolve everything for you."

Louella was at a loss for words. But since the police had cordoned off the area as an active crime scene, she didn't think she needed to stay there any longer, unless, of course, the police needed her for further questioning. But she was unable to decide where to go from there. She wished her mother was around to stand with her. The shock was unbearable. As soon as she found a place to sit, she sat down only to develop a strong urge to stand and pace up and down the pavement. Then she sat on the same spot again, stood up, and paced up and down until she was thoroughly exhausted. She wanted to scream but couldn't. She tried laughing but couldn't do that either. She put her hand on her head and tried to pull her hair. She was restless and needed help . . . urgently. Then she blacked out.

It took about five seconds for the officers to realize Louella was lying motionless on the concrete floor. One rushed to her, while the paramedics, who had been there all along came running and took over from the police officer. They were unsure whether she had passed out from what was unfolding before their eyes or whether an underlying condition caused her to faint. As a precaution, they rushed her to the emergency room. Unfortunately, she didn't have any next-of-kin to supply them with the information they needed. Her pulse seemed normal, but her blood pressure was dangerously high. She had been lying there for about three minutes before she opened her eyes. The emergency room lights blinded her eyes even though, under normal circumstances, they were not really that bright.

"What happened," she asked. "Where am I?"

"Shhhh," said the emergency room nurse as she tried to calm her down. "You were brought in here by the paramedics. But you need to rest while we work on you."

"Wait," Louella said, "I'm in the hospital?"

"Yes, you are," the nurse said. "You passed out and they brought you here to the emergency room."

It all started coming back slowly—her shop, the vandalism, the flowers all over the floor, then her pacing up and down. She appeared more confused and started wondering what hospital the paramedics had taken her to. As she was thinking through all these things, she started feeling sleepy. She hadn't slept much anyway, or perhaps it was the pain killers. And that was the last thought in her mind before she drifted off to sleep.

12

"HI, BOSS," MASON SAID over the phone. "Mission accomplished."

"Good job!" Mr. Dupree said. I hope you left no traces behind that could lead the bad boys to us."

"Everything's taken care of." said Mason. "Louella was brought to the scene, but she passed out and was rushed to the hospital."

"What hospital?" Mr. Dupree asked.

"Rockville Regional," Mason replied.

"Good." Mr. Dupree said. "You know what to do next. Be sure to take Sam along with you. A bouquet of flowers with a get-well-soon card will point all suspicion away from us."

"Copy that," said Mason. "I'll make sure to do it as soon as I get the chance."

"Don't wait too long. She might leave the hospital before you get there."

"I'll make sure to go while she's still there." Mason replied.

"Also, make sure you offer to underwrite the cost of rebuilding. No strings attached is the catchphrase."

"I'll do that, sir." Mason replied.

At daybreak, Mason called Sam. Sam was surprised to learn that Louella was in the hospital, and he was also unaware of their involvement in the vandalism. At any rate, Mason invited Sam to tag alongside him on his way to see Louella.

"Of course, I'll come along." Sam replied. "When do you wish to go?"

"As soon as yesterday," Mason replied. "We must find her in the hospital, and I'm sure she'll be worried about her business. Perhaps we can offer to rebuild it at no cost to her, and possibly leverage that to revisit the offer initially presented to her."

"You're a genius," Sam said. "I'm coming right over."

When Sam arrived at Mr. Dupree's office complex, Mason was in his office; Dupree wasn't. They exchanged pleasantries. They even told each other a few jokes. Then the tone of their conversation got a little more serious. They needed to act fast before any of the events that had happened at Rockville's Finest Flowers overtook them, so they both jumped into the Jeep Wagoneer belonging to Mr. Dupree's company and headed for Rockville Regional Hospital. After parking the car in the hospital's huge parking garage, they went down the elevator to the first floor, stepped out of the garage, and walked toward the emergency room's entrance.

They found themselves at the front desk of the emergency room.

"Hello," Mason started. "We're here to see Louella Goodman."

"May I have your names, please?" the front desk attendant asked.

"Absolutely! I'm Mason Kruger. This gentleman is Sam Palmer."

"How are you related to Louella Goodman?" she asked.

"We are friends of hers," Sam responded.

"Okay," the attendant replied. "I'll need your driver's licenses, please."

Both Sam and Mason pulled out their IDs from their wallets and handed them over to the attendant who then scanned them into her computer.

She handed their documents back to them and said, "Go down the hallway and turn left. Louella is in room 105."

"Thank you very much, ma'am," Mason said.

They both hurried off down the hallway and turned left into room 105. Louella was still in the room. It was around 8:23 am. She was surprised to see them this early.

"Well, isn't this a surprise!" she said. "How did you even know I was here?"

"Word travels fast," Mason said. "For one, it's in the news. Action News ran the story at 6 am, at 7 am, and I think it also ran it at 8 am. We might be lucky to see it again if we wait long enough."

Louella was not entirely eager to see the state of her business premises featured in the news, so she said, "I'll pass on that one. I've seen enough of it already."

They handed her a bouquet of flowers and a get-well-soon card, both of which they bought from a grocery store on their way to the hospital, the very store where Louella had seen Sam with Nancy.

Louella was moved by this act of kindness and expressed her deep appreciation to them, but she was more concerned about getting her business back on track. She was losing money by not opening, and the damage to her premises wasn't helping the situation one bit.

"Listen," Mason said, "as a gesture of good will, Mr. Dupree has offered to underwrite the cost of repairing your business premises. You don't have to pay him back for anything."

"Oh no! You don't have to do this," Louella protested. "Everything in that shop was insured, and I'll be filing a claim to my insurance company to recover everything I've lost. I just need to get back there in time to make sure I have an accurate record of the damage."

"How about we do that for you while you stay in the hospital?" Sam offered. "Taking care of your business in the state you're in should be the last thing on your mind right now."

"I might be able to let you do that," Louella consented. "What I won't do is have you cover the cost of repairing my shop. The insurance will take care of that. That's why I pay them all the premiums."

"Fair enough," Mason said. "If you don't mind, then, please let us head out to the scene and see if we can be of help."

"Sure. Not a problem at all." Louella said.

Mason and Sam left Louella at the hospital and headed for downtown Rockville to see the damage caused by the vandalism to Rockville's Finest Flowers. As they headed out, they reformulated a plan to get Louella to reverse her decision of dropping Mr. Dupree's proposal. How could they leverage the vandalism to their advantage? That was the question they asked themselves as they found their way to the shop.

13

Pastor Matthew was sitting in his study, looking at the sermon text for next Sunday's sermon. *Pray for Louella.* This thought came into his mind. He looked up from his Bible, a little surprised by the thought. He looked down again at his Bible to continue reading the text. *Pray for Louella.* This time the thought was almost audible. He wasn't sure what to make of it. He remembered how Louella had read the Scriptures the previous Sunday, and she had done a really good job, but what did that reading of Scripture have to do with the urge to pray for Louella?

Feeling a little embarrassed that he was acting on a thought that came from who knows where, he still put his Bible aside and began to pray for Louella. He wasn't sure what to pray for or even how to pray for this member of his congregation, but he decided to pray. Besides, it's never sinful to pray for anyone anyway, so he bowed his head and began praying.

He prayed the following prayer: "Lord, I'm not sure I know why the thought to pray for Louella came to my mind right now. However, if she's in any kind of situation that needs divine intervention, please send your angelic hosts to protect her from harm. Please come to her rescue. In Jesus' name I pray. Amen." He then felt the urge to call Louella. He picked up his phone and dialed her number.

"Hello," came a male voice at the other end of the line. "Are you looking for Louella?" Pastor Matthew's named appeared on Louella's caller ID, but the person who answered the phone played it safe, not wishing to appear as if he knew the caller's identity.

"Yes sir!" Pastor Matthew answered. "Where is she?"

"Well," said the voice, "before I answer, who might you be if I may ask?" He knew it was Pastor Matthew, for he'd heard him speak many times before. But for security purposes, he knew he had to confirm that Pastor Matthew was, indeed, the one calling.

"I'm her pastor," Pastor Matthew replied. "What's going on?"

"Louella's shop was vandalized this morning. I went over to her house to get her to come to her shop and see the damage for herself, and perhaps help us with the investigations. When she got here, she got so overwhelmed by what she saw, at least that's what we think, that she passed out. The paramedics rushed her to the emergency room at Rockville Regional Hospital. She's receiving treatment there as we speak."

"Lord, have mercy!" said Pastor Matthew. "Thank you very much for this information. I'll go over there and pray with her right away!"

As he drove off the parking lot, Pastor Matthew called his wife and let her know he was on his way to see Louella. It took him about 25 minutes to get to the hospital's emergency room. At the front desk, they gave him directions to Louella's room. In less than two minutes, he was knocking the door to room 105. Without waiting for an answer, he stepped into the room. There lay Louella with a one-inch bruise on her elbow. It was a fresh bruise, and it seemed to have been caused by Louella's fall.

"Louella," Pastor Matthew began, "so sorry for what's happened to you! How are you feeling?"

"Pastor!" Louella was finally excited to see someone she really wanted to see. "I'm so glad you came. How did you find out? I understand from Sam and Mason that the story about my shop is on the news?"

"Sam? Which Sam? The one I saw at church on Sunday?"

"Yes, that Sam. He was here with Mason. Mason is Mr. Dupree's attorney."

Pastor Sam sounded somewhat concerned about one of the two gentlemen Louella talked about. But he said, "Believe it or not, I didn't hear about this from the news. I was just sitting in my study, and something told me to pray for you, so I prayed, and when I finished praying, I called you. A policeman answered your phone and told me what happened. He said he stopped by your house to alert you about the vandalism in your shop."

That's when Louella remembered her phone, "Oh my! I don't have my phone. I must have left it in the car, along with my purse as well. Would you kindly go down there and ensure my stuff is safe?

"Of course!" Pastor Matthew said. "But before I go, let me pray for you one more time. I'm now convinced that voice was the Lord telling me to pray for you." Taking hold of Louella's hand, Pastor Matthew went down on one knee, asked the Lord to protect Louella, and prayed passionately for her safety. When they said their "Amens," the pastor wished her a quick recovery, excused himself, left the hospital, and headed for Louella's flower shop. He was somewhat speeding but kept calling himself out, reminding himself that speeding wouldn't change much. He then called his wife and asked her to bring one more member of Rockville Community Church with her and meet him at Louella's flower shop because he needed her to help him take some of Louella's stuff back to her house.

Upon his arrival, he found the policemen still walking back and forth around the crime scene. Two other individuals were there who seemed to wield some influence with the policemen, though one of them was a lot quieter than the other. Pastor Matthew immediately recognized the quiet individual—Sam. The other gentleman was quite talkative, and he seemed to be familiar with the legal issues surrounding the flower shop. Pastor Matthew assumed that he was the person Louella referred to as Mason. The pastor, however, called Louella's number again, and the same policeman picked it up. He soon learned that the pastor was there, and they linked up immediately.

"Pastor, thank you so much for coming," said the policeman. "We have everything under control.

"My pleasure. Is there any way I can help?" the pastor asked.

"The investigation is still in its early stages," said the policeman, "and we can't divulge any information at this point because we don't want to jeopardize the investigation. But Louella's lawyer is here and is helping us handle the legal issues."

That comment from the policeman made Pastor Matthew very uneasy. Rockville Community Church had a rocky relationship with Mason Kruger in the past. The church hired Mason as their legal representative when they tried to purchase their current piece of property where the sanctuary stood. However, the money disappeared into hands unknown, and the situation caused untold suffering and friction among a variety of church members. Some withdrew their membership and joined other churches. The pastor, at that time, resigned. For a while the church didn't have a pastor. After a period of about two years without a pastor, Pastor Matthew interviewed for the job and got it.

After learning that Mason was Louella's lawyer, the Pastor was not sure that Louella had made a good decision to hire Mason. But then, he was also not sure of the nature of Louella's relationship with Mason. Louella didn't tell him anything about hiring a lawyer to handle the issue either. Louella might just have given him a verbal go-ahead during Sam's and Mason's short visit with her at the hospital. Pastor Matthew looked for Louella's car and made sure everything was in order.

Pastor Matthew's wife, Sharon, arrived together with Julie, Mr. Smith's wife, the elder. Both Sharon and Julie gasped at the sight of all the mess they saw inside the flower shop. Sharon wasn't a frequent visitor to this shop, but every now and then, Louella's flower shop supplied the church with flowers on special occasions, including Easter, Veteran's Day, July 4th, and Memorial Day weekends, and Sharon had stopped by to pick them up. What she saw was heartbreaking. With tears in their eyes, Sharon and Julie picked up Louella's stuff and put them in her car. After chatting for a little while, they both decided to head back to Louella's house. Julie drove Louella's car while Sharon followed closely behind her. Upon their arrival at Louella's house, they put everything in the garage, lowered its door, locked the car, and headed to the pastor's house. However, they took Louella's phone and purse with them, hoping that they would head out to the hospital later in the day. It was a dramatic morning, more dramatic than any one of them could remember.

14

WHEN PASTOR MATTHEW GOT home, he found Sharon waiting for him at the door. No one else was at home except her. Their boys were in school. Sharon gave her husband a "welcome home" hug and inquired about Louella. After giving her the update, he expressed his concern about Louella's apparent hiring of Mason as her lawyer. He wasn't sure what to make of it. He just felt in his spirit that something wasn't right with that arrangement.

After talking for a while, Sharon assured him that if there was anything wrong with that arrangement, the Lord would make it plain to them. His job was to be a spiritual guide to Louella. Perhaps it would help him stay out of her business. Pastor Matthew saw the sense in that piece of advice and decided not to worry about it anymore.

Meanwhile, Sharon and Julie went to visit Louella at Rockville Regional Hospital. Since traffic had picked up some momentum, the commute to the hospital took slightly longer. Sharon and Julie weren't in a hurry, though, so the delay in traffic didn't bother them that much. As they traveled together in the same car, they chatted for a while. First it was about Louella's situation, about the church, about politics, about Louella again, and then back to the church. The more they talked, the shorter the commute felt. In fact, they were beginning to enjoy one another's company so much that they almost regretted it when they pulled into the parking lot of the hospital and stepped out of the car.

Once they got to the front desk, they asked to see Louella Goodman. The attendant took them through the usual drill of getting their driver's licenses and their street addresses.

"Louella is in room 105," they were told. "It's down the hallway. Turn left and you'll see Louella's room."

"Thank you," they said almost in a chorus and started off toward Louella's room.

As soon as they went through the door of her room, Louella's excitement upon seeing them was evident. She let out a loud but short scream. They both hugged her like siblings who haven't seen each other for a while, and they stayed in that tight embrace.

"I'm so sorry for what you've been through these past couple of hours," said Sharon.

"Can you imagine?" Julie exclaimed just as much as she was asking.

"This hurts," said Louella. "It really hurts. I'd made significant progress. It'll be hard to recover from the vandalism. I hope insurance covers everything I've lost."

As they were talking, they heard a voice. "Knock, knock," she announced herself. "It's the nurse. I'm here to check your vitals again."

Sharon and Julie stepped aside and observed as the nurse did her routine check-up of Louella.

"Everything seems okay," she said. "You've stabilized very well. I'll call the doctor for a final evaluation. You might be able to go home today."

"That's great news," said Louella. "I don't like staying in hospitals. I'd rather be in the comfort of my own home."

"I understand," Julie said. "This has been tough on you. I hope you get to rest completely once you get home."

Suddenly, Louella remembered she'd set up an appointment to interview a potential assistant. She let out another short scream, which startled Julie and Sharon. They thought something was wrong.

"What is it?" they asked.

She replied, "I set up an appointment to interview someone who was interested in becoming my assistant. Clearly, it's not going to work."

"Of course, it won't work," Sharon said. "Here, we brought your phone and purse. You can call the candidate and reschedule."

Louella was deeply grateful to both Julie and Sharon for bringing her phone and purse to her. A lot had fallen through the cracks since she passed out, and she thought she needed to make some calls to update those concerned about her situation.

"Louella," Sharon said, "You need to rest. You can't try to accomplish everything from your hospital bed. I think you should have someone help you with the phone calls."

"Well, that person wouldn't know what to say," Louella protested. "But resting, I will. You can take that to the bank."

Louella managed to make a few calls concerning her business. She also noticed a few missed calls, one of which she didn't recognize. She returned the call, and it turned out to be the person she was going to interview for the position. She gave the applicant a quick update of what was going on. One could tell that the person at the other end of the line was dumbfounded. She was watching the events unfold on Action News. At first, she didn't know that the news was about Louella's flower shop until she paid closer attention. They agreed to touch base when the dust had settled, and Louella hung up the phone.

She continued her conversation with Sharon and Julie, but before they could talk any further, Louella's emergency room doctor arrived. He looked at her vitals, asked her a few questions about how she was feeling, and went through what seemed like his standard routine involving cases of this sort.

"Well," the doctor said, "you seem to be showing no serious symptoms that would require you to stay here overnight. It would be safe to say you can go home today. I'll sign your discharge papers, and you'll be on your way. Please get plenty of rest." Turning to Sharon and Julie, but still addressing Louella, he said, "I hope you have family who can take you home." He turned back to Louella and said, "Like I said, please get plenty of rest. I wish you all the best."

And turning again to Sharon and Julie he said, smiling, "Nice to see you ladies." He then left the room.

"Likewise," they both said in a chorus.

"He's such a kind man," Sharon said. "I hope they were good to you."

"Oh, they were great," Louella replied. "But I'm ready to head home. I hope they discharge me soon. Will you guys give me a ride home? I don't want to use a taxi."

"We'd be honored to take you home," Julie said. "I'm glad we came just when they were preparing to discharge you."

"Me, too," Louella replied.

It didn't take long before the nurse brought in the discharge papers for Louella to sign. She then put her in a wheelchair and wheeled her all the way to the front door. Meanwhile, Sharon went to get the car so she could meet Julie and Louella at the door. Julie helped Louella get into the back seat of the car, and they were on their way to Louella's house.

It had been quite a morning for Louella, and the afternoon seemed perfect for her to catch up on some much-needed sleep. She'd been awake since 3:39 am, and her body was screaming for some rest. She listened. Once she got home, she went straight to bed and slept soundly. For how long, she couldn't remember, and, quite frankly, she didn't care. She just needed to rest. When she woke up, it was around 3 pm Thursday afternoon. Meanwhile, Sharon and Julie prepared a meal for her so she could eat later and left her to rest.

15

MASON AND SAM WENT back to Mr. Dupree's office complex. They found him waiting for them. Eager for some information, he asked them, "Well, what did you find?"

"The boys executed the plan just as we had asked them," Mason said, which took Sam by surprise.

"I don't understand. What are you talking about?" Sam asked.

"The flower shop," Mason replied. "It was all a plan to get Louella to return to the negotiating table."

"Are you talking about our visit to the flower shop this morning?" Sam's ignorance of the plan was evident. "And how is our visit to the shop supposed to bring Louella back to the negotiating table?" asked Sam.

"You will supply the missing piece of the puzzle," Mason replied.

"And exactly how am I supposed to do that?" Sam asked.

Gleeful about Sam's ignorance of the vandalism, Mason replied, "If you recall, you and Louella were hitting it off quite well. She was beginning to like you until she saw you with Nancy and things went sour between you and her."

Sam blushed and said, "Holy moly! I didn't know you knew about that brief altercation."

"I have my ways and means," Mason replied. "But we can try and set you two up again. Perhaps if she likes you, she might be able to like your uncle and then buy into the game plan."

To be sure, Sam was growing fond of Louella and really wanted to develop a deeper relationship with her. But Louella knew about Nancy.

"And what about Nancy?" Sam asked.

"Well, we'll keep Louella thinking she's your cousin just like you told her on Sunday," said Mason.

"What if she eventually finds out that she's not my cousin?" Sam asked.

"Oh, by then it'll be too late," Mason replied cunningly. "She'll already be exactly where we want her to be."

Sam was beginning to get really concerned, "And where would that be?" he asked.

Mason was intentional and deliberate with his answer: "Without her business, without a boyfriend, and without a home."

"And who will own that business and her home?" Sam asked, almost throwing up with disgust but doing everything he could to hide it.

"Your uncle, Sam. Your uncle. Of course, that also means I get to have a piece of the pie as well, since I've been doing your uncle's dirty business for him."

"Hold it!" Sam said, as if to command his uncle's lawyer to stop. "My uncle is a churchman. He goes to Rockville Community Church. He's a godly man. He wouldn't do this to a fellow church member."

"Church? My foot! I go to church, too. I'm a member of Rockville Community Church myself. I just don't go there that often because I work on Sundays."

"Oh no you don't," Sam countered. "You can't get away with this that easily."

"And what will you do?" Mason taunted. "If you try to file a police report, your uncle has contacts there, and it could get quite ugly for you. And since I know you love your uncle very much, you wouldn't want to tell on him, would you?"

Sam didn't know where to begin. He'd struck a great chord with Louella. He didn't know that he'd be caught in a scandalous trap that would cause her the sort of harm unfolding before his very eyes. Surely there had to be a sense of decency left, however remote, in Mason.

"Tell me something," Sam continued. "You say you're a member of Rockville Community Church. When did you last attend service there?"

"Easter Sunday," was the terse reply.

"Easter?" asked Sam. "I'm wrestling with my belief in God and I go there more regularly than you do. Are you even a believer in God?"

"We're all on a journey, searching for truth wherever we may find it. Sometimes I find it in church, and sometimes I don't. Moreover, I've had a negative encounter with the pastor of Rockville, and that makes me not want to go there that frequently anyway."

"*The* pastor? Are you talking about Pastor Matthew?"

"No," Mason replied. "I'm not talking about that pastor. I am talking about another pastor before Pastor Matthew came. But Pastor Matthew, obviously, knows the story. Someone in the church filled him in on it."

"Mind telling me what happened?" Sam asked.

"To be quite frank with you, Sam," Mason said, "it's none of your business."

"Of course, it's not, but who would trust you, considering the kinds of dealings I'm seeing you trying to execute?" Sam said.

"Go easy on me. It's not that bad. So are you in or are you out? Mason asked.

"Concerning what?" Sam asked.

"Louella?" Mason replied.

"What exactly do you want me to do?" Sam asked.

"Pretend you have a crush on her so she can fall for you." Mason replied.

"Listen, Mason," Sam said, "I'm interested in pursuing a relationship with Louella, Nancy's flirting with me notwithstanding. But I want it to be on my terms, not yours."

"So," Mason went on, "you're telling me you'll be pursuing a relationship with her on a serious note? Because if you do, that's all we need. You don't even have to talk with us again about it. Your uncle and I will take care of the rest."

Sam was really interested in Louella, but Nancy, whom he deceptively told Louella was his cousin, was also tugging his loyalty toward her. He knew he had to decide between Nancy and Louella. If he went for Nancy, then he'd better come clean with Louella and tell her Nancy isn't his cousin. But that would ruin whatever is left of his reputation. If he goes for Louella, then he has to come clean with Nancy and let her know he's no longer pursuing her, which still puts him at risk because Nancy might spill the beans on his dealings with Mason and his uncle.

Nancy was a waitress in a restaurant on the west side of Rockville—a restaurant run by Mr. Dupree. The restaurant was originally registered under Nancy as Nancy's Niceties. Mr. Dupree was impressed by Nancy's culinary skills. Being the CEO of Nancy's Niceties, she ran it like it was her own business specifically because it was her own business. It had succeeded tremendously, catching the eye of Mr. Dupree. He decided to give her an offer to buy the business and pay her double the monthly profit she was getting out of that business. In a meeting with Mason and Sam, Nancy saw the business proposal, similar to the one Mason had submitted to Louella. Nancy absolutely loved it and took the offer. During that meeting and subsequent meetings, Sam developed feelings for Nancy. Moreover, since she knew that she didn't have to work for her daily upkeep like she did before, she had more free time. Mr. Dupree was hoping to see a similar dynamic play itself out with Louella. It turned out, however, that Louella was more principled than Nancy, and that fact was infuriating Mr. Dupree, because he found Nancy somewhat naïve. He believed his influence was too forceful to be turned down. The very fact that Louella, a woman, was turning him down drove him up the wall. Hence, he devised the scheme to arm-twist Louella into surrendering Rockville's Finest Flowers to him.

What Louella didn't know was that Mason was behind the vandalism of her shop. She walked into the trap of allowing Mason to visit her vandalized shop to talk to the law enforcement officers, pretending to be her lawyer. From the time the crime started, Mason had watched at a distance from a secluded place as everything unfolded. Earlier, Mr. Dupree had urged Mason to hire the criminals and have them vandalize Louella's business. It was his way of retaliating against Louella's refusal to accept the business proposal and possibly grind it to a halt. He watched them wreak havoc all over the building and saw them leave the scene as soon as the burglar alarm went off. He watched as the squad cars and the fire trucks rushed to the scene about three minutes after the incident. He watched Louella arrive, driving behind another police car and saw her step into her business premises clearly distraught. He watched her sit and stand and pace up and down the walkway after talking to the detective, clearly dejected, until she passed out on the pavement. When the paramedics took her to hospital, he followed closely behind them until he saw them wheel her into the building. Then he drove to Mr. Dupree's office complex and called Sam to lay out the plan to visit her without revealing to Sam his involvement. He laid out the plan.

16

Early Thursday afternoon, two young men were having a drink near Jones Bank inside a bar called *Stay Sober*. They were playing pool as patrons came in and out of the pub. They seemed to be having the time of their lives. As they knocked the balls with their cues, one of them said something that caught Rick Mulley's attention: "Hit that ball like you did the flower shop this morning!"

Rick happened to be one of the plainclothes detectives handling Louella's business vandalism. He wasn't sure he'd heard it right, but he paid more attention to see if he could hear additional information.

"Come on, Bro! You know I didn't do it alone," the other man said. "You were right there with me."

"Let him who is without sin cast the first stone," the first spoke again.

"Of course, Larry! We're all in this together," came his friend's reply.

Detective Rick walked over to the two gentlemen and struck up a conversation with them regarding a completely unrelated topic. Since he was in street clothes, they didn't know he was a policeman. He couldn't believe his luck. He was working closely with the other detective assigned to Louella's case. He wanted to get their names and possibly figure out what cars they were driving so he could run their license plates on the division of motor vehicles database. In this way, he would know where they lived.

The two men weren't willing to talk much, but they talked enough for Rick to know that the first one was called Hank and the second one was Larry. Rick then stepped outside and stood at a convenient spot to see if Hank and Larry would get into their cars. His plan was to follow them safely at a distance but close enough to get the police department to run their license plates. He was successful with one of them—Larry. The department sent him Larry's address. Immediately thereafter, a search warrant was issued to inspect Larry's house.

When the cops arrived at Larry's house, they showed him the search warrant. He confidently let them in, being absolutely sure of his innocence. He complied with every request they made and passed with flying colors. They asked him to give them a detailed account of his whereabouts that day. Everything seemed to check out quite conveniently for him, including his alibi. However, he began to lose confidence when they asked for his phone. The detectives knew that if he had anything to do with the vandalism, quite likely, his phone records would give him away. He wasn't ready to part with his phone.

Eventually, however, the police acquired the permission to obtain the phone records. Most of the texts were brief messages to unknown recipients. Two text messages caught their attention. They seemed to have been sent to two individuals with the following content: "Mission accomplished." The reply came back with the following message: "Funds delivered." They traced the owner of the number, and it went back to Mr. Mason Kruger, the lawyer who spoke to them that morning as Louella's legal counsel! The other text message was traced to Mr. Dupree. He'd been included in the conversation between Mason and Larry.

Larry was asked to explain what the texts were all about. What mission were they trying to accomplish? Larry refused to divulge the information. It was confidential, he insisted. How much were they paid for the task? Larry refused to cooperate on that point as well. Once again, the detectives got permission to have the bank release their records concerning Larry's bank account activity. It showed an incoming wire transfer of five thousand dollars. Larry had some explaining to do. They also started going after Mason and Dupree.

Unfortunately, they hit a dead end. Nothing in the texts went beyond what they could plainly see. The more they prodded Larry, the harder it was for them to squeeze any piece of information from him. They decided to shelve the exercise for the evening and, perhaps, return to it the following day. It had been a long day for the detectives, and Rick was merely stopping by the pub to visit with a friend of his. Perhaps he was wrong in thinking Larry and Hank were responsible for the vandalism. The lead he got that afternoon seemed promising, and he thought he had cracked the case, but he seemed to hit a dead end with it. Still, he wasn't discouraged by the outcome. He'd dealt with different cases in the past and knew persistence often bore fruit for any detective work. As he headed home, he remembered Louella and how she'd been rushed to hospital. He thought of calling her to find out how she was doing but then decided against it.

He was also familiar with Mr. Dupree who was very well connected. Rumor had it that he had even wrapped the police chief around his finger. If that was the case, then this investigation perhaps wouldn't go too far. Still, Rick hoped justice would prevail and that hardworking citizens like Louella would eventually get the justice they deserved. He only hoped that if Larry and Hank were the masked vandals he saw on Louella's security video, he would at least succeed in tying them to the crime.

One more lead could prove fruitful. The brick the vandals used for breaking through the glass door of Louella's flower shop could possibly offer them some clues as to who threw it through the door. One such clue would be the vandals' DNA. If their skin, a strand of hair, or fingerprints could be found on the brick, or even on the cash register, the detectives would get valuable information leading them to the perpetrators of the crime. They would have to adopt a wait-and-see approach. Rick knew this case would take time to solve.

However, he was uncertain as to whether he'd break through the tight influential and corrupt network that Mr. Dupree had built throughout Rockville. His influence made prosecuting any criminals tied to him virtually impossible. Most of the judges were his puppets, having received huge financial bonuses from him. He was literally the owner of Rockville, and no one could outdo him in setting up an empire of the sort he was controlling. Rick knew how Mr. Dupree had gotten away with murder, literally and symbolically. What seemed to take more time to figure out was how he could break through the ranks of Mr. Dupree's puppets and bring him to justice without putting his own life in danger. This reality gave him sleepless nights. Perhaps, by cracking this case, he would finally bring Mr. Dupree to justice, but no one could know what the outcome would be—only God. At least that's what Rick thought, for he, too, like his pastor, Matthew, was a very devout man though, of course, he had his own weaknesses like everyone else.

17

Friday morning, a new day dawned, and Sam found himself in a dilemma, but he knew he had to recalibrate his relationship with Louella to set things straight. He found Nancy's beauty absolutely stunning. At the same time, he knew he could rely on Louella's spiritual maturity even though he wasn't quite drawn to spiritual things himself compared to her belief. Nevertheless, he convinced himself that a new day merited a new beginning, starting his relational life with Louella afresh. He picked up the phone and dialed Louella's number.

Louella was still asleep when the phone rang. When she saw Sam's name on the caller ID, she wasn't entirely thrilled, but she picked up the phone anyway because she needed to know what they saw when they returned to the scene of her flower shop.

"Good morning, Sam," she said.

"Good morning, Louella," Sam returned the greeting. "How are you feeling today?"

"I feel much better, thank you," Louella said. "How was your visit at my shop yesterday?"

"I was shocked by what I saw," Sam said.

"It really is quite shocking, isn't it?" Louella replied, and without waiting for Sam's answer, she went on. "Did Mason say anything out of the ordinary? I find him a little pushy."

Sam felt a little uncomfortable with Louella's question, but he braced himself and said, "He told the cops he was representing you in the matter and tried to leverage the cops to give him as much information as they could find."

"What?" Louella asked. "I didn't ask him to represent me. Did he identify himself or try to sign any papers?"

"Well, as a lawyer, he wouldn't sign any official documents without some proof from you to show the police."

"Did the police give him any information at all?" Louella asked.

"Not so far as I could tell," Sam replied. "But listen," Sam went on. "I think he was just trying to make sure things were running as they should from the law enforcement's end." Sam wanted to take the conversation a different direction, so he asked Louella, "If you're feeling better, I'd like to revisit the possibility of asking you out to dinner tonight. Would you be open to that?

"Sam, please give me time to recover fully. Physically, I'm doing well. I'm not psychologically at a place where I can meet with you tonight. I could do it on a different day, though."

"When do you think that might be?" Sam asked.

"Give me time to settle from yesterday's mess. It could take days or even weeks. I really don't know. I've never been in this situation before."

"Fair enough," Sam said. If he could get Louella thinking in that direction, he was at ease. But he didn't want her to know of his conversation with Mason. It could really mess things up for him. "Well, I hope things settle for you sooner rather than later," Sam went on.

"Me, too," she said. "As a matter of fact, I think I need to head out to my flower shop to see what's going on there. I haven't been there since passing out early yesterday morning."

"Is it okay if I meet you there?" Sam asked.

Louella felt she really had nothing to lose or gain by Sam's being there, so she said, "I'm okay with that. I need to get ready, though. I'll talk to you later."

"Wait," Sam said. "Before you hang up, what time do you think you'll be there."

"It's hard to say," Louella said. "I'll give you a call when I'm ready to leave the house. It takes about 20 to 25 minutes to get there, depending on traffic."

"Sounds like a plan," Sam said. "I'll be waiting for your call."

"Okay. Bye." Louella said and hung up.

"Bye," Sam said.

Louella fixed herself some cereal. She wasn't really in the mood for eating. The previous day's events gave her enough stress to kill her appetite, but she ate anyway. After getting ready for the day, she sent Sam a text saying she was leaving the house as she backed out of her driveway. Her phone dinged. It was a text message from Sam. He, too, was on his way. They both arrived at the flower shop at about the same time. As each stepped out of the car, they were both shocked to see Mason talking to the law enforcement officers.

Louella walked towards them and seemed concerned by how seriously Mason was taking this matter into his hands. Rick was also there. He remembered Louella. He had seen her at church when she read Scripture, but he didn't want to introduce that subject at this time. Furthermore, he wasn't surprised Louella didn't know he was a member of Rockville Community Church. A 300-hundred-member congregation, that's almost always full every Sunday, has the likelihood of strangers worshiping together and leaving immediately after the service. Rick was one such person.

He walked over to Louella and said, "Greetings, ma'am."

"Hello, sir," Louella replied. "How are you today?"

"I'm well. How about you? You took quite a hard fall yesterday," Rick asked and recalled at the same time.

"I feel much better physically. Emotionally, though, I'm not quite there yet. How far have you gone with the investigation? Have you found the culprits who did this?" she asked.

"Well, we've gotten some leads," he said. Then, pulling her aside to a private spot where he was confident no one could hear them, Rick asked, "Tell me something. Did you assign, verbally or otherwise, the legal aspect of the status of your business to Mason Kruger?"

"No, I did not," she replied. Pointing toward Sam's direction, who was standing about fifty yards away but certainly looking at them, she said, "Mason and that gentleman standing over there stopped by the emergency room to see me. They brought me a bouquet of flowers and a get-well-soon card. They then offered to come down here to see if they could offer any assistance. I told them I had no problem with that."

"Well, I don't know about Sam, but whatever you do, please be careful around Mason," Rick said. "That's all I can tell you right now."

What Rick told Louella began to confirm her fears that she might be dealing with a not-so-straightforward individual. She didn't know what to make of it. She asked Rick, "What should I do with him since he seems to be so interested in what's going on?"

"Leave that to me," Rick said. "I'll handle it."

"Oh, thank you very much," Louella said as they walked back to the flower shop's entrance. It was a beehive of law enforcement activity.

Uniformed police, detectives, and forensic experts were walking in and out of the flower shop. The do-not-cross tape was still in place. Nothing had been moved or cleared until all the pieces of forensic evidence had been gathered as much as they could. The shattered glass was still lying on the floor. The hustle and bustle of officers moving in and out of the premises indicated how seriously they took the matter. Louella counted at least two news station representatives positioning themselves for a live broadcast. The Action News van was parked about fifty yards away, and, not too far from them, a battery of journalists were trying to capture and cover as much of the story as they could.

Sam walked toward Louella and anxiously asked, "Well, is everything okay?"

"As much as it could be," Louella replied. But knowing that Sam and Mason had stopped by the flower shop the previous day, she didn't share with Sam about the warning she got from Rick about Mason. She thought it best to leave it unstated.

"Do you know if they have any leads or additional information as to who might have done this?" Sam kept pressing.

"The officer said they've found some leads, but they're keeping it under wraps in order not to jeopardize the investigation," Louella said.

"Ah, I see. I hope they catch the perpetrators soon," he said with uncharacteristic determination. He didn't like what Mason shared with him the previous day, and he hoped Mason's plan, whatever it was, would fall flat on its face. He really wanted to step into the flower shop to see the damage done, but that wasn't possible now. He decided to wait patiently for the go-ahead, but he wasn't sure when that would be. What he really wanted, though, was a moment with Louella, alone, for her to give him a second chance. He hoped that chance would come soon.

18

Rick drove the squad car back to the police station to work on the lead he got after Hank and Larry's comments. He strongly suspected he would link those two to the crime at Louella's flower shop. He was almost sure Mr. Dupree had played a role in this crime in some significant way. How significant, he couldn't quite tell. As he sat at his desk, he leaned back, putting the palms of his hands at the back of his head with elbows sticking out sideways, staring at the ceiling.

His boss dropped by his office and said, "Hi, Rick!"

"What's up, boss?" Rick asked.

"I hear you might have struck some leads in the flower shop case," the boss commented.

"I think I have," he said. "Two young lads at *Stay Sober* pub seemed to boast about a hit they made at some flower shop. That got my attention. I engaged them in a conversation, stepped outside to see what cars they drove when they left. I saw them jump into a Chevy Malibu. I sent the details of their plates to the DMV and got their street address. One of them, Larry, had texted Mason Kruger and Mr. Dupree about some mission accomplished, and they got payment for it.

"Here's what I want you to do," the boss said. "I want you to drop that lead."

"Excuse me?" Rick said, not sure if he heard the boss right. "What did you say?"

"You heard me," the boss said. "I want you to drop that lead."

"But sir, I am on the verge of . . ."

"Drop it! You hear me?" the boss said, raising his voice and storming out of the office.

Rick was surprised at the boss's insistence. He suspected Mr. Dupree's influence had penetrated the police department, but he didn't think it had gone this far. He owed it to Louella to ensure justice was done, so he stood up and followed the boss into his office.

"Sir," he said, "a serious crime has been committed. We must do everything in our power to bring the culprits to justice. We owe it to ourselves and to the victim to ensure it's not repeated. Why do you want me to drop this lead?"

"We have some very connected individuals," the boss said, "and they'll stop at nothing to fight off any attempts to arrest them. If Mr. Dupree is behind this, I can assure you, we won't be able to arrest him."

"With all due respect, sir," Rick continued, "we cannot allow lawlessness to rule over the police force. We have to fight back."

The boss looked at Rick, nodding up and down as if to say something, but uttered nothing. Then his words seemed deliberate and determined, "There is no fighting back." He said, "We can handle other crimes in this city, but we can't handle crimes where Mr. Dupree is involved. That's just the way it is."

Rick couldn't believe what was coming out of his boss's mouth. He'd been in that department for five years. This was the first time he was handling a case where Mr. Dupree was involved. He believed he would handle it as successfully as he'd handled other cases. But he was visibly surprised at how Mr. Dupree's case was being thrown out the window if, in fact, he was involved in vandalizing Louella's shop.

He returned to his desk and took a seat. Time seemed to go by rather quickly. His shift was ending in about thirty minutes. As he sat there, he played his conversation with his boss repeatedly in his mind. Something didn't seem to make sense. A lot failed to make sense. Before he knew it, the clock struck 1 pm.

"Time to go," he said out loud. "I'll see you guys tomorrow." He pretended to go home early, but in reality, he wanted to do further investigations on Louella's case. Since he didn't want to ruffle feathers, he had to pretend he was going home.

As he drove out, he noticed a familiar Jeep Wagoneer trailing him. From his rearview mirror, he could see Mason Kruger behind the wheel. *That's interesting*, he wondered. *A citizen trailing a detective*. He then dismissed the thought and kept driving. He decided to drop by *Stay Sober* again. *Possibly*, he thought to himself, *those young men are in there shooting pool like they did yesterday*. He walked in and took the same high table he'd taken the previous day. He looked in the direction where the pool table was sitting and thought he recognized one of the players. However, none resembled Larry or Hank, the young men he saw the previous day. This other familiar player didn't give him any reason to believe he'd be a person of interest in the case he was handling, which his boss had asked him to drop.

"Can I get you something?" asked the waitress.

"I'll go easy on myself today," he said. "Do you have any wine?"

"Sir, this is a place for beer and hard liquor," she said. "But let me see if we have any wine in stock."

In less than five minutes, she came back with a bottle and a glass of wine, saying, "Looks like today is your lucky day," as she emptied the bottle's contents into his glass.

"Thank you," said Rick, "though I have to admit I'm not as lucky as I would want to be."

"I'm sorry," said the waitress. "Things failed to pan out for you at work?"

"Something like that," he answered, "but I can handle it."

He picked up his glass and took a sip. He looked around at the tables again and took another sip. As he lifted his hand to take one more sip, his grip suddenly weakened, he blacked out and slowly went down to the floor like a noodle.

Someone sitting next to him screamed. Another said, "Call 911," after seeing him on the floor. Determining that Rick wasn't breathing, he began mouth-to-mouth resuscitation, he too felt dizzy and weak. Whatever was in Rick's mouth had transferred into the resuscitator's mouth, causing the exact same symptoms Rick was showing.

"What's in this drink?" asked one of the patrons, pointing to Rick's glass of wine.

"I gave him wine," said the waitress. "I didn't think it had something unfit for human consumption."

The ambulance arrived within minutes and found Rick lying there. They checked his pulse. He had no pulse. Word spread like wildfire. Not many knew he was a police officer until they found his business card in his wallet. They called Rockville Police Department with the news. In minutes, four squad cars were parked outside the pub. The paramedics were preparing to load Rick into the van. Meanwhile, the paramedics administered CPR, but shunned mouth to mouth resuscitation. The other gentleman who tried it on Rick was also receiving CPR, for he too had passed out and had no pulse. The ambulance rushed both of them to Rockville Regional Hospital. Perhaps Rick would survive the ordeal.

The policemen questioned the patron, asking her what she put in the glass Rick used.

"I tell you the truth," she said, "I didn't treat Rick any differently than I treat all my other customers. If I were to do this again, I would do it in the exact same way. How his drink took him down, I can't tell you. I'm surprised you considered me a suspect. Shame on you!" As she said that, she heard the back door of her kitchen close gently. She went to look and heard footsteps running away as fast as the legs could allow the runner. At the rear parking lot, a Jeep Wagoneer drove off considerably fast. The waitress couldn't identify the driver. She wondered who among the employees would be slipping out without letting them know. When she came back, the investigating officer picked up from where she left.

"We just want to get to the truth as much as you," they told her.

"I understand," she said. "You must do your work; I also must do mine. Otherwise, nothing will ever get done."

They took Rick's glass, put it in a Ziplock bag and sent it out to their lab.

Meanwhile, Rick's ambulance headed to the emergency room at top speed. He remained unresponsive. They wondered if they should call his time of death. When they finally got into the emergency room, the doctors worked on him. The chief doctor recognized him and ordered everyone out of the room. They frantically worked on him, possibly for thirty minutes, maybe less, maybe more. But it seemed as if they were too late. The doctor came out and shared the sad news with the team of officers seated in the waiting room. Without missing a beat, the doctor announced the dreaded news.

"He's gone. We called it at 1:55 pm," he said. "It looks like he died from potassium cyanide poisoning. His chances of survival were next to nil. We can't let you see him before we inform his next of kin. Fortunately, his emergency contact was in his wallet. We'll be sending a message to him momentarily." He then went back through the same door he came in and left them to process the information. As the doctor shut the door behind him, he suspected foul play and immediately called the FBI office in Lockridge. He was never at ease with recent happenings in Rockville, and this latest episode of the poisoning left him highly suspicious of what had transpired. He knew Rick quite well and was deeply troubled that he had to see Detective Rick in this way.

Meanwhile, word reached Rick's boss, Sergeant Drake Riley, that Rick didn't survive the poisoning. The entire department was in shock. That wasn't the way the day was supposed to end. The officers in that department loved Rick. At least that was the impression they gave him. Perhaps a line of duty death would be declared, giving Rick full honors. They wondered what Sergeant Riley would do about this.

19

LATE FRIDAY AFTERNOON, PASTOR Matthew was in his study when he heard a knock on his door. "Come in," he said.

It was his secretary, Alice Page. "Pastor Matthew," she said, "someone from Rockville Police Department is here. He says he has something urgent to tell you."

"Sure," he said. "Please let him in."

"Good morning, Pastor," the man said, "I'm Sergeant Drake Riley. One of our officers died unexpectedly yesterday. We understand he was a member of your church. His name was Detective Rick Mulley."

Pastor Matthew was shocked. "What? Rick Mulley is dead?"

"I'm afraid so, sir," said Sergeant Drake, "and as a department, we would like to ask you to do his funeral service. We've been in contact with his next of kin. Rick wasn't married, as you probably know. But his brother lives on the west side of Rockville. Pending approval from his brother, we think we'll be able to have his funeral next Wednesday. Would you be available to do it, and do you think we could use your sanctuary for the service?"

"That should be no problem," said Pastor Matthew, who was still trying to process all that information. Rick Mulley was one of his trusted congregation members. Owing to his status as a police officer, he kept a very low profile. But he was the same gentleman that alerted Louella about the vandalism of her flower shop.

"Would you mind telling me what killed him?" Pastor Matthew asked.

"At this point, we have no details about the circumstances that led to his death," Sergeant Drake said, "and if we did have it, we would more than likely withhold it from you until his immediate family is fully unformed."

"I understand," Pastor Matthew said.

"When can we meet to put the order of service together?" asked Sergeant Drake.

"Is Sunday, after our church service, a good time for you?" Pastor Matthew replied.

"That's doable. Sunday after church it is. See you then," Sergeant Drake said. After excusing himself, he stepped out of the office, walked to his car, and drove off.

"What was that about?" Alice asked. "Is everything okay?"

"I'm afraid not," Pastor Matthew said. "One of our members died unexpectedly yesterday."

"Oh no!" she said. "Who died?"

"Rick Mulley," he answered, "the rather quiet member of our church. He joined the church long before I got here. I didn't even know he was a police officer until very recently."

"My goodness!" Alice said. "I know Rick."

By this time other staff members of the church had gathered by the lobby just in time to hear Pastor Matthew share the shocking news. A solemn mood engulfed the small gathering.

After a deep sigh, Pastor Matthew said, "Let's pray."

They all agreed and, as if on cue, formed a circle and held their hands together. What followed was one of the sincerest prayers ever offered up to God at Rockville Community Church that Pastor Matthew could remember. Every person prayed, in turn, sometimes amid sobs, sometimes expressing shock, but every time believing without question that God was hearing their cry. And just as soon as it started, the mini revival at the lobby was over.

Pastor Matthew went back to his study to resume work on his sermon. As much as he tried, however, he couldn't get his mind to focus. He wondered how someone seemingly as healthy as Rick Mulley could ever be suddenly dies without explanation. The more he thought about it, the more it failed to make sense. He decided to set aside his books and take a walk around the church premises just to ease his mind for a while.

As he stepped out, his phone rang. It was Louella.

"Hi Louella," he said, "how are you?"

"Pastor," she asked, "What's this I'm hearing? Is Rick dead?

"I'm afraid so," he said.

"Dear God!" she exclaimed. "He was working on my case and now he's dead! Do you know how he died?"

"Well, the officer that stopped by said they don't have the details yet, and even if they did, they wouldn't reveal it to me until Rick's next of kin is informed."

"This is awful," Louella answered. "I really want to know how he died."

"So do we, Louella. So do we," the pastor said. "If I hear of anything and I'm allowed to share it, I'll let you know."

They ended the conversation, and Pastor Matthew started walking around the church premises. *Dear Lord,* he prayed, *please reveal to me what's going on. The enemy seems to be quite at work. Please protect your people in this congregation.* As he kept walking and praying, he tried to think of Scripture verses for encouragement. The more he walked around the church property, the more he was convinced he was dealing with some form of spiritual warfare. Spiritual warfare called for some periods of fasting. He wasn't sure he had the ability to endure another extended period of fasting. He had just come out of one several weeks ago.

His cell phone rang, and this time Sharon, his wife, was calling. "Honey, is it true?" she asked in desperation as soon as he picked up the phone.

"Yes, it is," he said.

"What are we going to do?" she asked again, getting even more desperate.

"Honey," he said, "just take it easy. I'm talking to the Lord about it. I'm walking outside the church building to clear my mind before I begin thinking of the way forward."

"Okay, dear," she said. "Do you need me to come over?"

"It would be great to see you," he said, "but you really don't have to come. I'll see you at 5 when I get home." They ended the conversation, and Pastor Matthew continued with his walk. Each day seemed to be getting more intense with one drama after another. He wasn't even sure the passage of Scripture he was thinking about for Sunday would be relevant in light of what had happened. The more he thought about it, the more he felt inclined to change it. He had sensed such promptings before. Sometimes the urge to change his sermons came minutes before he stood at the pulpit to preach. They happened to be the most frightening preaching experiences he ever encountered but, at the same time, the most powerful deliveries he gave. So what would the sermon be? He had no answer.

20

SERGEANT DRAKE CALLED JASON Mulley, Rick Mulley's brother, to inform him of his brother's death. Jason had already received the news with profound shock and sorrow from the doctor at Rockville Regional Hospital. Rick was Jason's elder brother, and he looked up to Rick in many ways. The two talked every week, sometimes spending their weekends together. Jason couldn't imagine a life without Rick. Rick was only a year and four months older than Jason. They looked like twins to many different people. Their resemblance was striking.

Jason had asked the hospital quite repeatedly to give him more information about his brother. He needed to know when he could go and see his body, which, as he was told, lay in the hospital's morgue. Since it was still a subject of investigation, the hospital was unsure of whether Jason would be allowed to see his brother. However, they promised Jason he would see his brother on Sunday, the day before the funeral, to say his goodbyes. Jason thought it wasn't a bad idea, after all. That was soon enough.

Chief Drake asked Jason to stop by the police department and get Rick's belongings from his desk, which they had cleared. Jason was happy to do so. When he arrived, three law enforcement officers waited for him at the entrance to the station. They led him all the way to Rick's desk. Sorrowfully, but keeping a stoic face, Jason picked up a small suitcase that contained Rick's papers, documents, pictures, and thumb drives. The officers showed him Rick's locker. His uniform was in there, neatly hanging inside, slightly above his well-polished shoes. Jason wheeled out the boxes and loaded them onto his truck. He returned for more items from Rick's locker. It took him three trips, finally, to clear Rick's desk and locker.

After clearing Rick's desk, Jason took everything to his house and decided he would go to Rick's home much later in the day. The drive to his house wasn't particularly long. In about twenty-five minutes, he was pulling into his driveway. His fiancée, Sally Greer, had stopped by to be with him as he mourned the passing of his brother. He got out of his car and walked into her arms, definitely feeling the pain of his brother's sudden departure. He was eager to know from the pathologist what took his brother's life. Jason checked his mailbox, which he had not done for about a week. A pile of envelopes was stacked in it, including some United States Postal Service priority mail. Jason wondered what the mail was all about. He held the pile of envelopes under his left arm and, with his left hand, held Sally's hand as they walked into Jason's house.

Rick was in pristine health. He had completed a half marathon the previous Saturday without a problem. He exercised daily and watched what he ate. He didn't smoke, or do drugs. He was a model citizen and, certainly, a model law enforcement officer. To be sure, he wasn't the only reliable police officer. A majority of the members of Rockville Police Department were upright, law-abiding police officers. That case couldn't be made convincingly of the police chief, however. As for Rick's health, the doctor gave him a clean bill of health after his annual physical. These facts made his death more surprising. He didn't die from an accident or from a heart attack. So what killed him? Jason needed answers and fast.

As he went through his brother's things from the office, Jason didn't know what to throw away and what to keep. He went through page after page of Rick's documents, including a certificate of excellence he received after a major drug bust on the south side of Rockville. He wondered why Rick hadn't put that certificate in a frame. He found a picture of Rick and him fishing by the lake outside Jason's house. A smile came to his face even as a teardrop rolled down and stained the picture. The more he went through the items, the more he missed his brother.

Jason was about to take a short coffee break before he decided to open the priority mail. It was from Rick, his brother. His heart raced as he found an old letter-sized brown envelope inside the USPS envelope. It didn't look like anything important, but two inscribed letters caught his attention at the bottom left corner of the envelope. The letters conveyed a message to Jason that took him by surprise. The writing was simple and in capital letters—BS. His heart began to throb faster. *BS?* I know what that means. It stands for bombshell. It was a sibling code word. They had agreed with each other that if anything ever happened to either of them, they would document, as much as possible, the information and put that information in a brown envelope with the inscription BS in the bottom left corner.

The envelope looked like it had been unsealed, resealed, and unsealed again. With trembling fingers, he tore it open and pulled out several sheets of paper and a thumb drive. They looked like phone records and bank records. The phone records showed text messages from two individuals—Larry and Hank—to Mason Kruger and from the same individuals to Mr. Dupree. Jason looked puzzled. But as he read the texts, he began to piece the information together. He forgot about Rick for a moment and began to make sense of the information. One Monday night group text from Mason to Larry and Hank read as follows:

> Mason: Hi, guys. I have an assignment for you that will pay handsomely.
>
> Larry, Hank: Really? What are we hitting this time?
>
> Mason: Rockville's Finest Flowers.
>
> Larry, Hank: When do we strike?
>
> Mason: Wednesday at 3 am.
>
> Larry, Hank; You got it.

Jason saw another text from Larry to Mason sent on Tuesday at around 5 am. The group text had the following message:

> Larry: Mission accomplished.
>
> Mason: Funds delivered.

Jason found it intriguing. What was all this about, and what did it have to do with Rick classifying it as BS? He saw another group text, and this time it included a Mr. Dupree.

> Larry, Hank: Misson accomplished.
>
> Masson, Dupree: Funds delivered.

Jason didn't know what to think of this, and Rick never shared with him much of what was happening at the police department. Jason saw another series of text messages between Drake and Dupree.

> Drake: Mission accomplished.
>
> Dupree: Awesome. Handsome reward coming.

Since none of these texts were making much sense to Jason, he looked inside the envelope again and saw a handwritten note. It wasn't addressed to anyone in particular, but it had the following message:

> My boss, Chief Drake, ordered me to stop investigating the vandalism of Rockville's Flowers, LLC. I was told not to continue with the investigation because a certain lead I had found seemed to link Mr. Dupree and Mason Kruger to the crime committed on the business premises. If anything should happen to me, let the reader understand that it's because I was beginning to uncover the crime that happened behind the scenes involving well connected individuals, including Mason Kruger, and Mr. Dupree. The bank records indicate that two young men, Hank and Larry, benefitted financially from the break-in at Rockville's Flowers, LLC. A recording of Chief Drake ordering me to stop the investigation is included in the thumb drive you'll find inside this envelope. Signed, Rick Mulley.

The contents of that letter hit Jason like a ton of bricks. He dug into the envelope one more time and saw bank records indicating a money wire transfer from Dupree Enterprises into Larry Gray's account in the amount of $5,000 and into Hank Davis's account also in the amount of $5,000. Jason Mulley's whole body was sweating and trembling. His brother was murdered, possibly by Drake himself. But how?

Sally was downstairs fixing lunch as Jason rummaged through Rick's belongings. He came running down the stairway from his bedroom, breathing heavily and sweating profusely.

"Honey," he told his fiancée, "look at this!"

Sally took the documents from his hands and began to read them, one by one. The more she read them, the paler she got.

"Oh my God!" Sally barely whispered, covering her mouth. "Rick was murdered. Shall we call the police?"

"Absolutely not," Jason said. "We don't know who the rotten apples are in that force. I want to go to Rick's house and see if I can find more information there."

"I'm coming with you," she said, and off they went. As they drove, Jason told her how they had formed a pact between them that if anything should happen to either of them, they would document everything and put it in an envelope with the inscription BS on it. That's how he knew Rick was murdered. It didn't take them long to get to Rick's house. As they stepped out of the car, something didn't look normal. Jason always had a spare key to Rick's house, so he opened the door, but the lock was already broken. As they stepped inside, they were shocked to see everything in a mess: broken plates on the kitchen and dining room floor, chairs upside down, chests of drawers open, and on and on. Someone was looking for something, but whatever it was, he or she couldn't find it. Jason and Sally backed out of the house slowly and, once outside, ran to the car and drove off at top speed. They both sensed that their lives were in danger. Jason wasn't sure where to go next as they drove back to his house. He wrestled with himself about his next move. He had a hard time figuring out what options he had. Should he call the CEO of Rockville's Finest Flowers? He wasn't sure about that move. She was as much a victim as Rick had been except that Rick's situation ended in death. Perhaps, he thought, that might be the wisest move under the circumstances. When they got home, they both agreed to talk with Louella.

21

Louella woke up on Saturday morning as worried as ever. Her shop had been vandalized. Her detective had been killed. Her church was in mourning. She felt as if her life was crushing her. She was afraid of everything. She thought the whole world was coming after her. As she sat on her couch, she mustered the courage to walk out to the mailbox and see whether she had any mail. She had not picked up mail for almost five days.

When she opened her mailbox, it was full. Most of it was junk mail. A significant portion included her electric bill and her utility bills. She also thought she might have seen her phone bill in the mix. As she went through her mail, she saw another letter that caught her attention. When she opened it, it reflected a mortgage bill twice the amount of what she owed her mortgage company, except that this was a different financial institution.

"That's funny," she muttered to herself. "I distinctly remember paying my mortgage bill last month. Why has it doubled?"

She went online into her mortgage account. It did indicate that she had paid her bill on time, and her next bill was on the first of the coming month, just as she had expected.

"What is this amount being asked of me?" she wondered. Since the bill included a number to call in case she had questions, she called it immediately. She was put on hold, and it took a while before someone answered. Finally, a voice at the other end of the line introduced herself as Amanda and offered to answer any questions she had, reminding her that the conversation was being recorded for quality purposes.

"Yes, Amanda," Louella said, "I'm calling you regarding a bill I'm holding in my hand about a mortgage bill I received. Would you tell me what it's all about?"

"Absolutely," Amanda said. "Would you read for me the account number appearing on the top right-hand corner of the bill?"

Louella read it out loud to Amanda who confirmed the number to Louella by reading it back.

"That's correct," Louella said.

"Give me a moment to look it up," Amanda said, "and then I'll get back to you."

"Certainly," Louella said. She was put on hold with classical music playing in the background. It didn't take too long before Amanda came back on the line.

"Hi Louella, are you still there?" Amanda asked.

"Yes, Amanda," Louella said.

"It appears, according to what I've found," Amanda went on, "that you signed up for a new mortgage this past Monday with our bank three weeks ago. This is just your first bill to be paid on the first of next month."

"That's a mistake," Louella replied. "I haven't signed up for any mortgage. In fact, I have a different mortgage company with Jones Bank and not you."

"Our records indicate that your current property is under our mortgage. If you think this is a mistake, you'll need to file a complaint with our resolutions department. I'm happy to link you up with them, but today is Saturday. I doubt you'll find anyone to help you at this time."

Louella didn't know whether to laugh or cry. No matter how hard she protested, Amanda was very sure that she had a mortgage separate from the loan she took out with her Jones Bank. She grew weak in her knees and almost fainted again. She couldn't call her pastor because her pastor was dealing with Rick's death, and she wasn't sure she wanted to dump her financial woes on him. His job is strictly spiritual not financial. She hung up the phone and cried and cried and cried.

She needed someone to talk to. She desperately needed somebody to hear her out. She found herself reaching out to Sam. She looked him up from her contacts and dialed his number.

"Hello."

"Hello, Sam," Louella said.

"Hey, Louella," Sam said. "What a pleasure to hear from you. How are you?"

"I'm not doing well," Louella replied.

"Why, what's going on?"

"A lot's been going on," Louella said. "The detective working on my case died on Thursday."

"What?" Sam asked, audibly surprised. "He died?"

"Yes, Sam. He died. And I just found out that I now have a second mortgage that I'm required to pay every month, and it's more than double the amount I pay for my current mortgage. Sam, I didn't take out a second loan. I have no recollection of doing that at all. Someone is trying to take my home away from me."

"That sounds ridiculous, Louella," Sam said. "Who would do such a thing?"

As he asked the question, Sam paused immediately and remembered Mason Kruger's words: "Without her business, without a boyfriend, and without a home." *Oh my goodness*, he thought, *Mason might be behind this! On the one hand he's pretending to help Louella, but on the other he's making good his threat.* Sam was sure Mason had gone to the county offices and had taken out a loan using Louella's home and title as collateral and making Louella pay for it. It seems to fit the pattern of Mason's intent.

"Sam?" Louella asked. "Sam are you there?"

"Yes, I am," Sam answered.

"Why did you go quiet on me?" she asked.

"I was trying to imagine what might have happened to get you into this situation," Sam answered. "It's very possible someone took out a loan under your name and is making you pay for it."

"But who would do such a thing?" Louella asked.

Of course, Sam knew the answer, but he wouldn't speak out since Louella knew that they often met and discussed her. That would put Sam dangerously close to Mason, and Sam was uncomfortable with that.

"Any bad person could have done it," Sam responded, and repeated, "Any bad person could have done it."

"Is there a way we can find out who the person is?" Louella asked.

"I can't think of any right now," Sam said, though he knew he wasn't being truthful, but went on, "Give me time to think of a possible solution."

Louella was surprised at how vulnerable she had become, but she had nothing more to lose at this point, so she said, "By the way, I'm open today for an evening meal if you're available."

Sam took the chance and said, "Of course I'm available. Same place, same time?" he asked.

"Sure! I'll see you then," Louella said and ended the conversation.

22

No sooner had Louella ended her conversation with Sam than her phone rang again.

"Hello," she said.

"Hello, is this Louella?" asked the person at the other end of the line.

"How may I help you?" replied Louella.

"Hi, Louella, this is Jason Mulley. I am Rick Mulley's brother."

"Oh!" Louella responded in a tone of sympathy.

"Is it possible to meet up with you for a conversation? I have something I wish to run by you," Jason said.

"When do you want to do this?" Louella asked.

"Can we do it this evening?" replied.

"This evening is not good," said Louella. "I've made some plans."

"Well, how about tomorrow?" Jason asked again.

"Tomorrow isn't good either," Louella responded. "I want to go to church, especially tomorrow. I need to be in church."

"Well, can we meet after church?" Jason asked. "It's really important that I talk to you."

"I guess I could meet you after church," she said, as if she was giving in to Jason's pressure.

"What church will you be going to?" Jason asked.

"I go to Rockville Community Church," she replied, "and that's where I'll be tomorrow for service."

"That was my brother's church," Jason Mulley said somewhat shocked that his brother Rick attended the same church Louella attended. "I should say this is, indeed, a small world."

"He was a member of Rockville, but he kept a very low profile at the church," Louella noted. "Perhaps he didn't want too much attention owing to the nature of his job."

"That kind of work requires one to be extremely careful," Jason said. "So," he went on, "what time does service begin?"

"It begins at 10:30 am," she replied. "You might need to come early. It fills up really fast."

"Okay," Jason replied. "Thanks for the heads-up," and hung up the phone.

Louella heard the disconnecting beep in her cell phone, and she hung up as well. She started preparing herself emotionally for the day in the hope it would get better than it was really sounding. Still, she wondered what Jason wanted to share with her. She wondered if she would have a better day had she met with him today rather than tomorrow, which was Sunday. She felt, in her heart, that it wasn't fair for her to schedule a meeting on the Lord's Day, but since she had done it already, she decided to go with the plan.

The day went by really fast. She wanted to talk with Sam. She was hoping he would help her make sense of what had happened to her the past few days. Even though he seemed somewhat untrustworthy, she believed he was the best shot she had under the circumstances to help improve her day by, perhaps, giving her positive ideas of how the day could get better, or figure out how she could fight the financial institution putting her home into a second mortgage she didn't sign up for, or practical solutions for helping her business take off, or possible ways she, too, could go to the gym to establish a more elaborate fitness regimen—anything but negativity would be welcome.

As she kept thinking of all these possibilities, her time with Sam was quickly approaching. She had a grocery list of questions lined up for him. She wasn't sure which of the questions would come first, for they weren't really listed, in her mind, in the order of preference. As she thought about her upcoming dinner meeting, she started heading toward the car. Perhaps she would begin driving early to avoid having to speed on the highway. Having any run-ins with the law at this stage of a stalled business would only be applying salt to her already wounded soul. The drive to Town House Coffee was smooth and efficient without much traffic on the road. Before long, the green roof of the coffee house appeared. She soon found herself pulling into the parking lot. It was almost empty. She looked at her watch. It read

4:12 pm. *What! She thought to herself. I'm here too early. What will I do all this time waiting for Sam?* She decided to browse the Internet on her phone as she waited for him. First it was Facebook, then Instagram, then Tik-Tok, then X, then back to Facebook. She got bored with that. She decided to go directly to different sites on the web. Even there, she got bored, so she decided to play online scrabble. This would certainly help her kill time. By the time she completed a couple of games, she thought, it would be time to meet with Sam.

She looked up because she thought she saw, out of the corner of her eye, a familiar truck pulling up beside her. It was Sam. He too came early and was visibly surprised to see Louella there already.

"Whoa," he said as he opened the door and got out. 'Talk about getting here early! I thought I'd beat you to the clock.

"I'm surprised you're here early," she said. "It looks like today was a slow day for you."

"You're right," Sam said. "I had no wedding planning gigs today, and I am really delighted and honored you called me. Please feel free to do so whenever you want to talk."

"I certainly will," she said, "and especially today, I really want to talk."

"Well, let's go in and talk over coffee," he offered.

"I think that's a good idea," she obliged. "No need to wait until 5 pm."

Sam opened the car door for Louella, and she stepped out of the car gingerly. She then went ahead of him and, looking back, slowed down enough for him to walk by her side. Once they got in, a few waiters and waitresses seemed to recognize them, but vaguely.

As they were led to their seats, Louella couldn't wait for them to be seated.

"Well, Sam," she started, "this has been quite a tough week. I even feel guilty that I'm out here having coffee and not trying to solve the problem with my shop."

"I'm all ears," Sam said. "Talk to me."

"I'm in danger of losing my business. I'm in danger of losing my home, and. at this rate, I'm in danger of losing my health!"

"Easy now," Sam said, "things aren't as bad as they seem."

"How worse could they get than this?" Louella said.

"Well, you're a woman of faith," Sam offered. "Perhaps you would benefit from some higher power at this point."

"You don't really believe in that yourself," Louella said as if to protest.

"I'm on my own pilgrimage just like I told you when we first met right here in this coffee house," Sam reminded her.

"I've been doing a lot of praying," Louella said. "I draw a lot of strength from that. Pastor Matthew has been delivering some really powerful sermons. Do you ever pray at all?"

"Like I said," Sam answered, "I'm on my own spiritual pilgrimage. When I arrive at the truth, I'll be more than happy to share it with you."

The conversation kept going back and forth about spiritual matters. Louella wanted to reignite the conversation about the recent happenings in her life, but she did wonder how she could put a positive spin onto those unfortunate events. Perhaps talking about spiritual matters, about her faith, and about God would be positive enough.

Sam, however, wasn't very keen on discussing faith matters. He didn't think faith rested on solid scientific evidence, but he was open to the possibility that perhaps, at some point in the future, the postulates of all this spiritual stuff Louella was talking about would be scientifically verified. For now, he was merely content with the fact that a very respectable woman sought him out, expressing her need for him. Perhaps this would be a good time for him to initiate a move that would take their friendship to the next level, his crush on Nancy notwithstanding.

"I was thinking, Louella," he said.

"Yes, Sam," she offered.

"I've admired your strict ethical principles, and you'd be the kind of person I'd like to know more," he said.

"Wow, Sam," Louella said. "You seem to be suggesting something more than your words convey."

"You're right," he said, "and I wonder if I could see you more frequently."

Something happened to Louella, the exact feeling she got when Sam first walked into her flower shop. She knew she liked Sam, but something stopped her dead in her tracks. Nancy. Then she remembered what Sam said: Nancy was his cousin. Those familiar feelings reignited.

"Well, Sam," Louella said, "so much is happening to me right now. I'm not sure I'm ready to jump into the kind of commitment you're suggesting."

"Here's what I suggest," Sam said. "I'm here for you when you need me, just like you called me to talk to me today. I felt honored by that invitation from you. Besides, you need someone to lean on in situations like this."

"You're right," Louella said. "It's maddening not having someone to talk to when one goes through what I'm going through." The more they talked, the more Louella realized she was drawing closer to Sam emotionally and psychologically. In addition to looking well-built and handsome, perhaps he wasn't a bad man after all. Just like their first meeting at Town House Coffee, their discussion went well into the evening. Before they realized it, they were the only customers left as the employees began cleaning up the tables and setting up for the next day.

"Oops," Louella said, "I think we should call it a night. Thank you so much for the evening. It felt good not having to talk or think about my woes for a while."

"Well, thank *you*," Sam said. "I was honored to be there for you."

"I'll see you around," Louella said. "I'll be in church tomorrow. You're welcome to come. Pastor Matthew is a really good preacher."

"Tell me about it," Sam agreed. "But I'll stay at home tomorrow and prepare for the funeral service on Wednesday." The funeral! Louella had forgotten about the funeral. That reminded her she would be meeting with Rick Mulley's brother, Jason.

"Ah, yes!" She said. "Rick Mulley was working on my case. I can't believe he's gone. I think I'll attend the funeral. I guess I'll see you on Wednesday, then."

"Yes, ma'am," Sam said as they got up from the table to head to their cars. The moonlit parking lot was bright enough for them to see their reflections on Louella's car. Sam opened the door for her. Louella extended her hands around him to give him a goodnight hug. He hugged her back and gave her shoulder a double pat, double rub, and double pat before wishing her good-night. She thanked him for the evening, got into her car, turned on the ignition, and drove off. It was a better night for her than most of the nights that week.

23

SUNDAY SERVICE AT ROCKVILLE Community Church was packed. Word had spread like wildfire that Rick Mulley had died. Among those attending the service was Jason Mulley. Jason had heard a lot about Pastor Matthew from his brother, Rick. He wanted to hear Pastor Matthew speak. He especially wanted to hear him preach an ordinary nonfuneral sermon. He showed up early, true to his promise to Louella, and found himself a convenient seat closer to the front of the church but certainly not the front seat. He sat there and observed the faithful walking into the sanctuary. They seemed to know each other quite well. A lot of them, however, were speaking in low tones, whispering, nodding, and throwing their hands into the air. A few of them were weeping possibly because they were hearing for the first time about Rick Mulley's sudden death.

Jason saw someone wearing a clerical collar coming into the sanctuary through a door on the right side of the stage. He assumed at once that this was Pastor Matthew. The man walked toward a chair located at the center stage, set his books on the table beside the chair, tested his microphone to see if it was working, and then walked down the stage to strike a conversation with members of the congregation. He seemed to know almost everyone in attendance. Those he didn't know, he intentionally introduced himself to them and sought to know who they were. He then walked toward Jason Mulley who was sitting quietly on the center row a few pews behind the front.

"Hello, sir," Pastor Matthew said, "welcome to the service today. I'm Pastor Matthew."

"Hello, Pastor Matthew," said Jason. "Very nice to meet you. I'm Jason Mulley, Rick Mulley's brother."

"Oh! Jason! I am so glad to meet you, and I'm truly sorry about your brother," Pastor Matthew said. "Did you travel from out of town?"

"I actually live on the west side of Rockville," Jason said, "but I decided to come to church today to experience what Rick knew every Sunday."

"It's so kind of you to come," said Pastor Matthew. "What an honor to meet you!"

"Rick always talked about you," Jason said. "He had nothing but great things to say."

"Bless him," said Matthew. "I'm still coming to terms with the fact that he is no more on this side of heaven, though, of course we believe he is with Jesus."

"Me, too," Jason said, his voice trailing off and choking in grief and sadness.

Pastor Matthew took Jason's hand with his right hand and patted his back with his left as if to say, nonverbally, what both could have said to each other but were too overwhelmed to say it.

After giving Jason an assuring nod, he said, "Welcome to the service, sir. I hope I get to see you later."

"Of course," Jason said. "Blessings to you, sir."

Pastor Matthew moved on to other members, shaking a hand here and giving an assuring hug there, throwing a well-meaning remark at some mischievous teenager pulling a prank on him just to get his attention and then high fiving him. More people walked into the sanctuary—young folk, senior citizens, widows, families, nursing mothers, and people in wheelchairs and using walkers. Jason wondered how the pastor kept up with such a wide variety of congregants. Then he answered himself: *that's why they go to seminary*. That settled it for him.

Jason wasn't sure whether Louella was in the service until he heard Pastor Matthew's voice. "Louella," Pastor Matthew said, "welcome. Am I glad you are here today!"

"Thank you, Pastor," Louella said.

"Here," Pastor Matthew said as he walked toward Jason, "I have someone I'd like you to meet," and getting Jason's attention he said, "Jason, this is Louella Goodman, the owner of Rockville's Finest Flowers. Your brother was working on her case."

Turning to Louella, Pastor Matthew said, "Louella, this is Jason Mulley, Rick Mulley's brother."

Jason stood up and took Louella's hands with both of his, saying, "Louella, it's such a pleasure to meet you."

"I'm so sorry about your brother, Jason," Louella said.

Jason decided not to make it obvious to Pastor Matthew that he was also there to see Louella. He kept that bit of information under wraps. But as soon as Pastor Matthew moved on to speak with additional arrivals into the sanctuary, Jason furtively passed on a brown envelope to Louella. He hoped no one had seen him do it.

He then said in a whisper, "Please read the contents of that envelope as soon as you get home."

Not knowing how to handle the situation, Louella decided to play along and said, "Sure!"

As soon as she said that, Jason thought he saw a frightening faced man walk into the sanctuary through the narthex. It was his late brother's boss, Chief Drake Riley. He immediately sensed danger. *Jees! I hope he didn't see me*, Jason thought. Not knowing whether he was safe in the sanctuary or not, he immediately looked down and turned his back toward Chief Drake who was looking around the sanctuary, trying to find a place to sit. The sanctuary was already packed, and the ushers were quickly running out of space to seat additional guests. They led Chief Drake toward Jason. *Oh no!* Jason thought. *They're bringing him over here. He can't know I'm here.* The usher seemed to be rushing toward Jason, as if he knew Chief Drake was looking for Jason. When he got to Jason's pew, the usher walked right past him and found him a spot three pews in front of Jason but to the left of the aisle on the adjacent row. *Phew! That was close!* Jason thought to himself. *I need an exit strategy to walk out of here before he sees me.*

Service began with a prelude from the pianist. Pastor Matthew then went up to the podium and made the sad announcement about Rick Mulley's passing. Jason shed a tear as he remembered his brother, but he was still too nervous to focus on the pastor's words. As their childhood memories came to mind, from their fights to their adventurous excursions in the nearby forest, to the time they nearly drowned while boating on the Rockville River, Jason was still preoccupied with the fact that his brother was murdered, possibly by Chief Drake. He couldn't believe Drake just went past him without recognizing him.

Pastor Matthew went on to describe Rick Mulley as a faithful and active member of Rockville Community Church and how he had relied on Rick on different occasions, including Rick's help with the investigation into the vandalism of Louella's flower shop. It had been a trying week for the church, Pastor Matthew observed. He had tailored the service to reflect the victory believers have in Jesus Christ. The hymns were uplifting. The Scripture reading was relevant. This time Jeremy Jones did the Scripture reading. Louella did the reading on Jeremy's behalf the previous Sunday because he was down with flu-like symptoms, but he looked strong today. His voice resonated with deep conviction.

As all this was going on, Jason sent a quick text to Louella. "I'll try my best to meet with you after the service," he wrote. "But if this doesn't happen, please READ the contents of that envelope and follow the instructions." Louella heard her phone buzz. She looked at it, read the message, looked at Jason from her sitting position, and nodded. Jason saw her out of the corner of his eye. She was texting back. He had silenced his phone. But he took it out and saw Louella's acknowledgement. Whatever Pastor Matthew said in his sermon went past Jason. Louella didn't pay attention to the sermon either. She sensed something was wrong with Jason.

"It's not safe for me to be here," Jason texted Louella back.

"What are you talking about?" Louella asked.

"Read the contents of the envelope. You'll understand," he said.

Louella seemed confused. How could Jason say he wasn't safe in church of all the places? If anything, church was the safest place to be. At least that was what she thought. Before she knew it, Pastor Matthew concluded his sermon. They sang the final hymn and, before giving the benediction, Pastor Matthew reminded the congregation about Rick Mulley's funeral, which would be on Wednesday, three days away. He even went ahead and acknowledged the presence of Jason Mulley, Rick Mulley's brother, in the congregation. As he did so, he looked in Jason's direction to point him to the congregation, and this gesture got Chief Drake Riley supremely interested. He even took a step forward and stood on tiptoe to get a better view of Jason, but Jason was gone, much to Pastor Matthew's surprise.

24

Chief Drake Riley didn't wait to shake the pastor's hand as the congregation normally did at the end of the service, though he had come to work on the order of service for the funeral. As the congregation exited the building through the church's main entrance, Drake rushed toward the side door with his radio in hand, giving unspecified instructions to his squad. Louella saw Chief Riley heading out through the alternate exit. She knew at once that he was going after Jason, going by the text she'd read from him. She went to one of the study rooms in the church and opened the envelope. She pulled out a letter that read as follows:

> If you're reading this letter, it's because I'm unable to tell you its contents in person. I'm absolutely sure that bad apples in Rockville Police Department are responsible for the death of my brother, Detective Rick Mulley. I've scanned all records confirming this allegation into the enclosed thumb drive. If by the time you are reading this it should turn out that I'm unavailable to talk to you, please hand this thumb drive to Action News and have them look at it. They'll know exactly what to do. Thank you. Signed, Jason Mulley.

Louella's heart was pounding so hard she feared it would give her away. Thankfully everybody was heading to their cars. As she stepped outside the study room, she heard Pastor Matthew's voice in the sanctuary. He had just finished shaking everyone's hand and was heading toward his study, which was two doors away from the study room.

"Pastor Matthew," she heard a voice calling him. "Would you know of a certain lady named Louella?"

"Yes, Chief Riley," Pastor Matthew said. "She's the owner of the flower shop that got vandalized."

"Right," said Chief Riley. "Was she in the service today?"

"Yes, she was," said Pastor Matthew. "As a matter of fact, I talked with her before service and even introduced her to Rick's brother, Jason."

"Aha!" said Riley. "Do you know if she's gone home already?"

"I don't remember shaking her hand as people left the building," said Pastor Matthew.

Immediately Louella knew she was in trouble. She already had important information from Jason, Rick's brother, and they were now looking for her. She slipped the envelope under the door of Pastor Matthew's study and tiptoed down the hallway toward the back exit of the building.

"There she is," said Pastor Matthew. "Louella! Chief Riley is looking for you."

Louella didn't wait to respond to Pastor Matthew. She kept going through the door, stepped outside, went round the building to the parking lot and ran toward her car, but she ran into the waiting hands of one of Riley's men who held her so tightly in their grasp that she could hardly breathe.

"The thumb drive, Louella," said the officer. "Hand me the thumb drive."

"What thumb drive?" Louella asked

"The thumb drive Jason gave you this morning in church," the officer said. "Hand it over now or you'll be arrested for interfering with our investigations."

"I don't know what you're talking about," Louella said.

The officers searched her bag and gave her a pat down. They didn't find any thumb drive on her. They went back into the sanctuary, but it was too big for them to know where to begin. In addition, there were several offices in the building with too many computers and thumb drives that it would take them a whole evening to comb through just one room. Not knowing what else to do, they gave up.

Pastor Matthew, presently, stepped out of the church building and saw Louella under police custody. Somewhat horrified that a member of his congregation seemed to be under arrest, he walked toward the policemen and asked, "Can anyone tell me what's going on here?"

"We think Louella, here, has access to some privileged information pertinent to our investigation," the police officer said.

"What investigation, officer?" Pastor Matthew asked.

"I can't tell you that," the officer replied. "It's privileged information."

"What's he talking about, Louella?" Pastor Matthew asked her.

"I don't know," Louella replied. "They don't even have an arrest warrant."

"Officers," Pastor Matthew said, "we've just had a wonderful service here. On Wednesday we will be burying one of your own. You haven't given me any reason why you're holding a member of my congregation, and you have no warrant for her arrest. Unless you can show it to me, may I kindly ask you to leave?"

Chief Riley finally caught up with them. After quietly consulting with the rest of his squad, he walked back to Pastor Matthew and said, "We'll let her go for now. But please know she's a person of interest, and we may ask her to accompany us to the police station when the time comes."

"Thank you, sir," Pastor Matthew said. "We thank you for your service to the community, but kindly leave us in peace. As it is, Louella is already distraught by the vandalism of her shop. Please bear that in mind. Meanwhile, I'll work on the funeral order of service and send you a soft copy by email. Please text me your email address, and thank you!"

"Oh, we know all about the vandalism very well," said Chief Riley. "But we'll see you on Wednesday at the funeral. Good day to you, sir."

"Good day to you," Pastor Matthew said, and the entire squad drove off.

25

"LOUELLA," PASTOR MATTHEW STARTED, "is there something I need to know?"

"It's complicated," Louella said. "I'm not even sure I understand it myself."

"What I need to know," Pastor Matthew went on, "is why an entire squad from the Rockville Police Department seems bent on sucking your blood right now!"

"It must have something to do with the envelope," Louella said.

"Envelope?" Pastor Matthew asked. "What envelope?"

"The brown envelope under your office door," she said.

"Under my. . .wha. . .have you been to my office?" Pastor Matthew asked.

"I slipped it under your door when I heard you and Chief Riley calling out my name," she said.

"What's in the envelope?" Pastor Matthew asked.

"I don't know," she said. "It must be some incriminating information."

"Where did you get that envelope?" Pastor Matthew pressed further.

"I got it from Jason, Rick Mulley's brother," she said.

"Wait a minute," Pastor Matthew said. "Within that short introduction you went as far as accepting an envelope from Jason, a person you just met today?"

"He seems to want me to do him a favor," she said, "and I'm just curious about the nature of that favor."

"Look, Louella," Pastor Matthew said, "you're have enough problems already. Why are you taking up more problems than you need?"

"Jason seems to know something about the police department, possibly related to his brother, Rick," she said.

"For starters," Pastor Matthew said, "let's walk over to my office to dispose of that envelope. It seems to be a major source of your woes."

"Oh, no! Don't!" Louella said. "I'll take that envelope. I promised to give Jason all the help I can as far as the information in that envelope is concerned."

"Well, let's find out what's in it," Pastor Matthew offered.

"You do know that if you see, read, or hear anything from that envelope, you become privy to the same information."

"Well, my sanctuary has been desecrated by an intrusion already, and I'm determined to clean it up," Pastor Matthew said. "If that means pulling out the contents of that envelope, then so be it."

They both hurried into the sanctuary and found a few bewildered remnants from the service trying to make sense of what they had just witnessed. One of them was his wife, Sharon, and his two boys. Sharon walked to him and locked her arms into his as they walked toward his office. She asked the kids to wait outside the office as they talked.

"Is everything okay, pastor?" they asked.

"We're all safe," he said. "I'm just trying to understand why the cops came into our sanctuary and behaved the way they did."

Pastor Matthew opened the door into his office and saw the brown envelope lying on the floor as he swung the door open. He picked it up. It was already opened and bulging from the thumb drive inside. He pulled out the thumb drive, plugged it into his desktop and clicked it open. Only one document named "my brother," appeared. Pastor Matthew clicked on the document. It looked like a pile of screenshots with the following contents:

> Mason: Hi guys, I have an assignment for you that will pay handsomely.
>
> Larry, Hank: Really? What are we hitting this time?
>
> Mason: Rockville's Finest Flowers.
>
> Larry, Hank: When do we strike?
>
> Mason: Tuesday at 3 am.
>
> Larry, Hank; You got it.

Another screenshot from Larry to Mason, sent on Tuesday at around 5 am depicted a text with the following message:

> Larry: Mission accomplished.
>
> Mason: Funds delivered.

Another screenshot depicted a group text, and this time it included a Mr. Dupree, whom Louella recognized immediately, though Pastor Matthew did not quite know him. It read:

> Larry, Hank: Misson accomplished
>
> Mason, Dupree: Funds delivered.

Another screenshot with an additional series of text messages between Drake and Dupree continued to baffle Pastor Matthew, his wife, and Louella.

> Drake: Mission accomplished.
>
> Dupree: Awesome. Handsome reward coming.

What seemed to explain the reason why Chief Riley was in a raiding mood was the following message:

> My boss, Chief Drake, ordered me to stop investigating the vandalism of Rockville's Flowers, LLC. I was told not to continue with the investigation because a certain lead I had found seemed to link Mr. Dupree and Mason Kruger to the crime committed on the business premises. If anything should happen to me, let the reader understand that it's because I was beginning to uncover the crime that happened behind the scenes involving well connected individuals, including Mason Kruger, and Mr. Dupree. The bank records indicate that two young men, Hank and Larry, benefitted financially from the break-in at Rockville's Flowers, LLC. A recording of Chief Drake ordering me to stop the investigation is included in the thumb drive you'll find inside this envelope. Signed, Rick Mulley.

The contents shocked Pastor Matthew. In consternation, his wife put the palm of her hand across her wide-open mouth. Louella was hysterical. She didn't know whether to sit, stand, cry, or laugh. She'd just gone through a similar episode when she saw her flower shop vandalized with shattered glass strewn all over the floor.

"Rick Mulley was murdered," Pastor Matthew said, half whispering and certainly crying, "and by his own boss!"

"They all seem to be Mr. Dupree's puppets!" Louella exclaimed. "We've got to call the police."

"Louella," Pastor Matthew reasoned. "Don't you understand? The police are involved!"

"There has to be someone in that department we can rely on," she said.

"Well, we really don't know how far Mr. Dupree's tentacles have reached," Pastor Matthew said. "What other information do we have here?"

"Jason said we should call Action News and give them this thumb drive," Louella said, showing Pastor Matthew the letter Jason included in the envelope.

"What if Action News is part of this scandal?" Pastor Matthew asked. "If Dupree can permeate the police department, he can permeate the TV stations."

"You could be right about that, but I desperately hope you're wrong, honey," Pastor Matthew's wife said.

"I'm scared," Louella whispered. "I don't know what to do."

"Perhaps you could go home and think these things over," Pastor Matthew suggested.

"That would be a good idea," Louella said. "But before I go, would you please pray for all this?"

"I would be happy to," Pastor Matthew said. "Let's pray." They bowed their heads as Pastor Matthew led them in prayer. He prayed for Louella's protection. He prayed that the truth would come to light and that the perpetrators of the crime would be exposed. He prayed that those perpetrators would develop a relationship with Jesus Christ. When the pastor was done, they all said in a chorus, "Amen."

But before they called it a day, Pastor Matthew remembered Jason. The more he ignored the thought of Jason, the more he felt an urge to pray for Jason, so he said, "Dear ones, you know Jason's brother, Rick, will be buried on Wednesday. The funeral service will be here. He's going through a very rough patch. Rick wasn't only his brother; Rick was his childhood friend. Let's pause for a moment and pray for Jason."

Holding hands, they prayed for Jason. First Louella, then Pastor Matthew's wife, and then the pastor himself, but he seemed to have a burden for Jason weighing much more heavily on him than on the other two. While holding their hands, Pastor Matthew went on his knees and prayed fervently for Jason. He prayed and besought the Lord for Jason's safety.

Meanwhile, the police had gone after Jason immediately after he had exited the sanctuary earlier. By the time they got to the parking lot, Jason was already taking the exit to the highway.

"Quick," one officer said, "He's getting away! Get into the car!"

They both jumped into the squad car and started after Jason. As soon as they got to the highway, they could see Jason's truck fading away into the distance round a gentle bend. The officers turned on their lights and stepped on the gas. They started inching closer to Jason. Suddenly, as they approached another bend, they saw Jason's truck taking an exit at top speed. It spun out of control, hit an embankment, flew off the cliff and flipped into the air before landing down, forty feet below, on the sand dunes by Rockville River. The officers slowed down, reached the spot of the accident, and parked their squad car at the edge of the cliff. They got out of the car and walked toward the edge. They could see the mangled wreck forty feet below with its wheels upside down, still spinning. They looked at each other, nodded, and got back into their car. One of them turned on the radio and reported an accident, giving the dispatch the car's exact location.

"We don't think the person made it out alive," they said as they drove away. "The car is pretty beaten up." Ordinarily, they would have stayed at the scene until the paramedics arrived. But they wanted Jason dead, just like they wanted Rick dead. For that reason, they couldn't care less that he might be dying. This was less trouble to deal with because it was one less person to worry about.

26

James Dupree was holding an emergency meeting with Chief Drake Riley. Tempers were flaring, and they were shouting at each other. No one really knew what the other was saying in the midst of all the raucous noise. Standing up, Mason Kruger decided to play the role of arbiter.

"Guys! Guys! Guys!" he shouted. "Please, one person at a time."

"Be quiet, Lippy," Mr. Dupree turned to Mason patronizingly. "Don't forget you work for me!" Immediately Mason abandoned his temporary role and sat down. The shouting match continued.

"You let Louella go?" Mr. Dupree's question roared.

"Yes, sir," replied Chief Riley. "We could find nothing on her."

"How dare you let her go!" he exclaimed in a loud voice.

"As I said," Chief Riley spoke through clenched teeth, "we found nothing on her."

"Are you sure she has nothing that would incriminate us?" pressed Mr. Dupree.

"If it's there, we couldn't find it," said Chief Riley. We ransacked Rick Mulley's house and found nothing.

"Well, what about his office desk?" asked Mr. Dupree

"We also cleared up the desk and found nothing there," said Chief Riley, somewhat agitated that Mr. Dupree asked him all these questions. He wasn't used to being grilled. He asked the questions not the other way round.

"Are you sure he had nothing in his desk?" asked Mr. Dupree

"His brother picked up all the stuff we had cleared from Rick's desk, the important stuff, the nonessentials, and the trash," said Chief Riley.

"And you're telling me he was at Rockville Community Church for worship today?" Mr. Dupree asked.

"Yes, he was," Chief Riley said.

"Well, why didn't you go after him?" asked Mr. Dupree.

"We did as soon as we saw him walk through the door. By the time my boys got to the parking lot, he left at top speed, so they went after him."

"Then what happened?" Mr. Dupree prompted.

"The chase ended in a crash. Jason Mulley's car flipped and fell off the cliff by Rockville River. There's no way he would have survived that crash," said Chief Riley.

"Well, did you verify his death?" asked Mr. Dupree.

"There was no way he could have walked out of the crash alive," said Chief Riley.

"Are you sure he's dead?" asked Mr. Dupree.

"Yes, sir. No one can take such a fall and survive," said Chief Riley.

"You can't be too sure," said Mr. Dupree. "I think we should send someone there to check it just to make sure."

"Are you doubting me?" said Chief Riley. "Why don't you let me do my job?"

"I'm helping you do your job," Mr. Dupree said.

"Well," said Drake Riley sarcastically, "I appreciate your concern. But stay out of the way and let me do my job."

"If you did your job," Mr. Dupree shouted, "we wouldn't be in this mess. I've given your department tons and tons of money and this is how you repay me—by not doing your job?"

"You and I know why you give us so much of your money," Chief Riley said and, poking Mr. Dupree's chest with his finger, he went on. "You want to get away with murder, literally and symbolically."

Completely angered by Riley's gesture, Mr. Dupree fist-grabbed Chief Riley's poking finger and wrestled it away from him, saying, "Get your hands off me! You know I can finish you off in a second."

"You forget, Mr. Dupree," said Chief Riley, "that we are the finishers. You pay us to do your dirty work for you. Who else will you ask to destroy us?"

"I have my ways and means, but don't you ever poke me with your finger again!" Mr. Dupree warned Chief Riley as if his word was the final one in the conversation. He then went on, rambling, "And if you can't do or finish your work, then let me know so I can find other people to do the job."

Meanwhile, Mason was quietly watching these two men go for each other's throats, as it were. He wasn't sure he liked what he saw, but he was impressed by Mr. Dupree's self-confidence. *This guy can move mountains if he wants to,* he thought. His influence got Detective Rick Mulley killed. Who knows what else he can do? No one kills a police officer and gets away with it.

"What about the girl?" Mr. Dupree asked, making reference to Louella. "When will you evict her from her house?"

"Why should I evict someone who owns her house?" asked Chief Riley.

"Well, not anymore," said Mr. Dupree. "That home now belongs to me. I transferred the title to my name from county records. Go and tell her to leave my house now."

"Wait a minute," Chief Riley said. "She lost her business, and now you're making her lose her home?"

"I'm not responsible for the loss of her business," said Mr. Dupree.

"Yes, you are," Chief Riley responded before Mr. Dupree could defend himself further. "Remember the thugs you hired to do your dirty job for you? They squealed on you."

"I wasn't there when it was happening," said Mr. Dupree, "so you can't say I vandalized Rockville's Finest Flowers."

"Well," said Chief Riley, "the texts you sent back and forth prove otherwise. I'm sure the phrase "Mission accomplished" means something very profound to you since you received texts with that expression."

Mr. Dupree's anger was at its zenith. He clenched his fist and swung his arm as if to punch Chief Riley in the face, but before he could do it, Mason restrained him by putting his arms around him tightly.

"Mr. Dupree," Mason warned, "assaulting a police officer is a felony. Control yourself!"

"In this region, I'm above the law," bragged Mr. Dupree. "No one can arrest me. I arrest people."

Chief Riley was getting really fed up with Mr. Dupree's self-conceit. Perhaps it wasn't a good idea for him to accept all the generous donations from Mr. Dupree. It helped fund some of the department's fundamental needs, but Mr. Dupree was using his donating power as leverage for getting whatever he wanted from the police. Chief Riley was beginning to learn his lesson. He should have kept police matters within the department. Mingling with the public was, perhaps, not a very good idea after all. Look where it landed him. But before he could cut links with Mr. Dupree completely, he had one more task to accomplish.

27

Jason lay in his car pretty stunned. Suddenly, he opened his eyes and was absolutely confused. The world seemed upside down. He had no idea where he was, and neither was he sure of how long he remained in that upside-down position. For a moment he wondered how he found himself in that that way. Then it occurred to him: the police chase, just like in the movies, except that for the movies, it was all make-believe. This was the real deal. He was in a serious accident from a police car chase, and he was alive. He had dashed out of Rockville Community Church after Pastor Matthew acknowledged his attendance and saw two officers coming at him once he got to his car. He was a wanted man. Now that he was in this wreck, how come no one was there to get him? He wondered about that.

He started moving slowly. He winced at the sharp pain coming from his knee. He felt as if he had fractured it. But he slowly and carefully pulled himself out through the broken window, with shattered glass all over the roof of the upside-down car. His muscles were sore, and his back felt like it was on fire. But he had to move fast and get out of the wreck quickly.

"Ouch!" he yelled. The sharp, torn and twisted metal found the flesh on his arm and tore it open as he moved his hands and legs to crawl out of the car. Blood began oozing out.

"Oh, great!" he said. "Now I have one more problem to deal with." He took off his shirt and tore off the back section. He then wrapped the torn-off piece around the one inch cut on his forearm. He believed the T-shirt he wore underneath was sufficient to keep him clothed from his waist up. He hated the idea of walking bare chested. Thankfully his pants were still intact. As he felt all over his body to determine whether he had broken any bones, he heard a siren approaching, getting louder with each second.

"I must get out of here," he said out loud. "I'm not sure whether those are friends or foe." He started limping away, feeling extremely sore. The sand by the river was dry and hot from the afternoon sun. He worried that his footprints would lead the paramedics to his location, so rather than walking along the riverbank, he decided to go up the cliff. He quickly realized that the forty-foot cliff was too steep to climb. He couldn't use the main road to gain his bearings. Furthermore, he wasn't sure his rescuers were really coming to rescue him. Perhaps they were Drake Riley's puppets. *Perhaps they were the puppets of Mr. Dup. . . Dupray. . . Dupree*, he thought through the possibilities of how that strange name would sound. As he tried to find a sure footing to get him up the cliff, he noticed something was missing—his phone. He couldn't leave his phone behind. It had crucial information he needed for the recent happenings.

"Oh great!" he said out loud. "Now I have to go back for my phone."

"You don't have to," said the voice of a stranger standing fourteen feet away from him. "I have your phone right here." Jason was startled. He thought he was the only person at the accident scene.

"Do I know you?" Jason asked.

"No, you don't." the stranger said. "But I saw your car fly in the air and flip several times before it landed upside down in the mangled wreck it's in now."

"Thank you for getting my phone," said Jason.

"Are you okay?" said the stranger. "You took quite a hard fall!"

"I believe I'm okay," said Jason. "I'm just hoping I have no broken bones."

"Is there a place you need to go?" asked the stranger. "I'm more than happy to take you there, assuming you don't mind."

"No, sir. I believe I'm okay," Jason said, not sure whether he really wanted to be on his own or whether someone needed to be there with him. He ran his hands all over his body one more time, looking for broken bones, just to assure himself he was okay.

"Suit yourself," said the stranger as Jason was still feeling around his knees and arms. "If you need anything, please call me. I'll be there immediately," the stranger added.

"Thank you very much, sir," said Jason as he looked up and stretched his hands to give the stranger a handshake. "I really appreciate your . . ." The stranger was gone. *Wait, it can't be. Where did he go*? Jason looked at where the man was standing. *He left without giving me his contact information*. He could see, from the sand, the imprints of the man's feet coming toward him from the car, and he wanted to follow the man to thank him. So he looked for his footprints to determine what direction he'd taken. Unfortunately, the only set of footprints he could see were the stranger's footprints toward him, showing the direction he had come from. The footprints clearly indicated where the stranger had come from and they ended exactly where he had stopped to hand over Jason's phone. They didn't go beyond that point. The stranger seemed to have vanished into thin air. He saw no footprints leading away from him that would have indicated the direction the stranger would have taken. Could he have come face-to-face with an angel and not even know it? He didn't even get to ask the stranger's name. The stranger was completely gone. How was he to call the stranger?

Jason started walking in the direction of his home. He was on the east side of town, but he wasn't sure whether he was heading east, west, north, or south. He just wanted to be walking along the road, hoping he would see a familiar landmark—one that would help him get back to his house. This was certainly a trying moment for him. He started walking, and walking he did. Every time he saw a police car, he looked down to avoid recognition. He'd been on the run since discovering the BS envelope given to him by his brother, Rick. He knew Rick was counting on him to bring the corrupt members of Rockville Police Department to justice. He thought he'd let his brother down by handing the envelope over to Louella. And by doing so, he'd taken a huge risk. He wondered if Louella had handed the documents over to Action News. It would have made quite a sensational story.

Then it dawned on him that he didn't have to keep trekking without knowing where he was going. A taxi would take him where he needed to go. But wait a minute. He also downloaded the Rider App on his phone. He could summon a taxi to his exact spot, and someone would come and get him. Thankfully, his phone was still functional. The accident didn't ruin it. He looked for the Rider App and opened it. His ride options were listed from the least expensive to the most expensive. At this point, any ride would do, so he selected the first one driven by a Mr. Stanley Kirkpatrick. From his phone, he could monitor Stanley's car's location. It started heading off in his direction. The estimated time of arrival would be five minutes—quick enough to get him to his house but perhaps not quick enough to keep him from getting spotted by any cops driving by.

In the meantime, he had to make sure he concealed his face. With Chief Drake Riley on the lookout for him, he was sure an alert had been sent to all units to arrest him. He also wanted to get in touch with Sally Greer, his fiancée. She had to know what happened to him, so he called her.

"Jason?" she asked as she answered the phone.

"Hi, honey," Jason responded.

"Where are you?" she asked again.

"I'm walking on the freeway here waiting for my ride to get me home," he said.

"What are you doing on the freeway?" she asked.

"It's a long story," he said, "but Chief Riley's men came after me in their squad cars and started chasing me as I drove my truck."

"Really?" she asked, absolutely stunned. "Then what happened."

"The truck flipped and flew over a cliff as I went round a bend on the freeway." It landed about forty feet below.

"Oh my gosh," she said. "Are you okay?"

"Yes, I am," Jason said. "But the truck is totaled. The cops left me alone, probably thinking I was dead or something."

"Jason, please be careful," she pleaded. "Those guys are nuts!"

"Tell me about it. And then a strange thing happened. I left the mangled wreck down the cliff, only to realize I'd forgotten my phone in the car. Someone I've never seen before followed me and gave me my phone. As I took a look at the phone to see if it was still working, the stranger told me to call him if I needed anything. I looked up to thank him, but he was gone. I mean . . . gone . . . completely out of sight. He disappeared into thin air. I could see the footprints his feet made when he walked toward me, but they ended where he stopped to hand me my phone. There were no more footprints after he vanished."

"Jason," Sally said, "You're going through a tough time. Let me know when you get home. I'll meet you there. Right now, I'm at my parents' house."

"Okay, dear," Jason said. "My ride is about to get here." His ride finally came—a Honda Civic, possibly driven by a college student wanting to make some extra pocket money.

"Is this Jason?" the driver asked, popping his head out of the driver's window.

"Yes, sir," said Jason.

"For security purposes, can you tell me who I am?" the driver asked.

"You're Stanley Kirkpatrick," said Jason.

Stanley jumped out of his car, opened the rear door, and let Jason in. He then got back into the driver's seat and simply followed the GPS to Jason's intended destination.

"Just to be sure," Stanley said, "we're heading to 105 Lefty Loop, Rockville. Is that correct?"

"You got it, sir," Jason said. Jason could see from the GPS that he was seventeen miles from his house. He was surprised at how quickly the police chase got him to drive seventeen miles away from town. But he was grateful for the ride. It would be, at least, twenty-five minutes of some much-needed peace. He wanted to take a nap, but he was too anxious to shut his eyes. He had to stay alert. One never knows when the cops would spot him, and he knew he had to stay low.

"You seem to have hurt yourself," Stanley said. "Are you okay?"

Jason was a little surprised by the question. He asked, "What do you mean?"

"Your arm," Stanley noted. "It's bleeding. You need to have that checked."

Jason was too preoccupied with finding a ride that he'd forgotten about his arm. Apparently, how he wrapped his torn shirt around the wound wasn't sufficient to keep the blood from oozing through.

"My goodness," said Jason, "I'd forgotten about this."

"What happened?" Stanley asked.

Jason wasn't sure he could trust someone he'd just met with what he knew already, so he gave a very shallow answer.

"Oh, this is just a tiny wound from a cut I got by the river," he said.

"Whatever it is," Stanley said, "you need to have that professionally looked at."

"I will," Jason said, relieved that Stanley wasn't getting too nosey. As they rode in silence, Jason thought about the stranger, his sudden appearance with Jason's phone, and sudden disappearance without leaving Jason with any contact, name, or address. That encounter seemed very odd. The fact that the stranger showed up just when he needed to get his phone seemed rather bizarre, but then again, nothing seemed normal at this point in light of all the recent happenings. He wondered what the outcome of the recent happenings would be—death? Vindication? Bringing Chief Riley to justice? He couldn't tell.

As they approached 105 Lefty Loop, Jason noticed a number of squad cars parked outside his home. Immediately he instructed Stanley to keep driving.

"Don't stop until I tell you to."

"But this is your home, right?" Stanley asked.

"You see all these cops here?" Jason asked, pointing to them one by one. "They're looking for somebody. We don't want to interfere with that." Actually, he sensed very strongly that whatever reason those cops had for being there, they had to be tied directly to him. He wasn't going to risk his safety by getting out of the car. When they went past his house, he noticed at least two of them standing outside his door.

"Keep driving until I tell you to stop," he said again. "When I find it convenient, I will let you know."

"I hear you," said Stanley, and he stepped on the gas.

After going three blocks, Jason said, "Okay. You can stop now." Stanley stopped the car.

"Wait here," Jason said as he stepped out. He carefully scanned the street with his eyes. Then he said, "I need to call my fiancée."

"Hi, honey," Jason said as Sally picked up the phone.

"Hi, dear," she answered. "Are you home now?"

"Not exactly. I'm standing about a hundred yards away from home. There's a bunch of cop cars outside my house. Would you know of anything that might be going on around here right now?"

"Jason," Sally started, "the only thing I can think of is that those boys are out to get you. I think you should lie low for a while. You and I saw all that stuff you found from your late brother's desk, especially the brown BS envelope."

"Yes, we did, honey, and I gave it to a certain Miss Louella to hand over to Action News in case anything happens to me."

"Come over to my parents' house and then we can figure out where to put you up for the night," Sally offered.

Jason felt uncomfortable about that offer but decided to go anyway. At this point in the game, he wasn't going to take any chances exposing himself to people who seemed to be after his own blood. He entered Salley's parent's street address into his Rider App and asked Stanley to drive him to the new location. Stanley wondered what all this was about, but it gave him some good business. He was only pleased to help out needy citizens, and more so if it brought him money.

28

After praying with Pastor Matthew, Louella decided to drive home. That day turned out to be one of the strangest encounters she'd ever had in her life. It happened in church of all the places. As she ran through the events of the day in her mind, she seemed unaware of how far she had driven. When she pulled into her driveway, she hardly recognized her own home. Several cars were parked outside, including a Jeep Wagoneer. A familiar silver-haired man was standing outside her house with members of the Rockville Police Department. Next to him was a person Louella had met before—Mason Kruger. Mason was the proposal writer, a proposal Louella flatly rejected. What on earth were they doing here? Louella's emotions began to plummet with panic. *Are the cops still coming after me, and what does Mr. Dupree and Mason Kruger have to do with all this?* She wondered as she stopped her car and stepped out.

One of the officers walked toward her and asked, "Louella Goodman, is that you?"

"Yes, it is. What's going on?"

"We have specific instructions by the owner of this home to evict you," the officer said.

"You can't evict me from my home," Louella said.

"Ma'am," the officer said, "this isn't your home. It belongs to Mr. James Dupree. He has the records to prove it, and he wants you to vacate this home." The officer showed Louella all the legal documents, including the title, already bearing Dupree Enterprises as the rightful owner of the house.

"NOOOOOOO!" Louella screamed at the top of her voice. "You can't take away my home! I am almost done paying off my mortgage."

"That's not what the records show, ma'am," said the police officer. "We give you four weeks to vacate this house. Otherwise, legal action will be taken against you, and you don't want that."

"I'm NOT getting out of my home," she said. "You, all of you, get off my property!"

"Not anymore," said Mr. Dupree, who had seen Louella pull into the driveway and began walking toward her. "It's not your property. This IS my house now." Mason was standing next to him taking notes of the conversation.

"How in the world could you even think this house belongs to you?" Louella demanded.

Mr. Dupree answered, "It's not that I *think* the house belongs to me. I actually *know* the house belongs to me. You have no home here. If you wanted to own it, you should have paid your mortgage. You have one week to leave. Otherwise, you'll be forcefully evicted and possibly prosecuted." Mason was still taking notes, never looking up, but seriously and furiously making sure nothing in the conversation was missed.

"How DARE you!" said Louella. "You know what you're doing is illegal. You're retaliating against me. I refused your offer to join your company, and you're punishing me by taking my house. How dare you!"

"No ma'am," said Dupree with a sinister smile, "what *you* are doing is illegal." With that he and Mason jumped into his Wagoneer, slammed the door shut, started the engine, and drove off. The officers began to drive off one by one. In less than a minute, she was left all by herself alone in her driveway. She couldn't believe what she'd just seen and heard. It was surreal. She wondered how she could be losing a home she'd taken so much pains to build and to own. What a tragedy. She decided to call Sam.

"Hello, Louella," Sam answered.

"Sam!" Louella screamed. "They're taking away my home! They're taking my home away from me, Sam! What am I gonna do?"

"Wait, hold on," Sam said. "What do you mean they're taking away your home. Who's taking away your home?"

"Your uncle, Sam. Your uncle is taking away my home!"

Sam felt an audible, painful twist in his intestines. Something was churning inside him. His uncle was taking away his friend's home.

"W-w-wait a minute," he said. "Are you sure? How do you know that?

"Mr. James Dupree himself was here, and he showed me the papers that legally confirm that my house is now his house, Sam. He has given me four weeks to vacate my home."

"That can't be."

"Yes, it can," said Louella. "Why are you finding it hard to believe this?"

"My uncle wouldn't do such a thing," Sam said, though he really mistrusted his own words. He knew his uncle had been privy to quite a number of shady deals. Taking someone's house wasn't entirely out of the question.

Louella went on, "I don't know how to fight this, Sam. Your uncle seems to have Chief Riley wrapped around his finger. His men were here less than five minutes ago, and they're ready to evict me from my home—a home I've taken pains to pay off. Did you know about this, Sam?"

"Of course not," Sam responded. "I knew nothing about this. But if it's true, then it is really tragic.

"What do you mean 'if this is true,' Sam?" Louella objected. "Do you doubt I'm telling you the truth? I'm telling you your uncle was here and gave me four weeks to vacate this place."

"Louella," Sam said, "I believe you. Let me call him and see if I can stop him."

"Would you, please?" Louella pleaded. "If you can do that, it could save me weeks, perhaps even months and years of fighting this in court."

"I'm here for you, Louella," Sam said. "Let me see if I can help you."

That conversation with Sam gave Louella a temporary sense of relief. She didn't know how she could handle the evening if she went to bed without a plan to fight the eviction she was being served. Who did James Dupree think he was by coming over to her house and taking it over? Surely the existence of law and order counts for something in the city of Rockville. That's what she thought and really believed. But recent happenings suggested to her that Rockville was degenerating into a state of lawlessness with no clear remedy in sight. As she thought through what was going on, she decided to call Pastor Matthew for spiritual strength.

Pastor Matthew picked up the phone and said, "Hello, Louella! How can I help you?"

"Hi, Pastor," Louella said. "Some members of the Rockville Police Department were here along with Mr. James Dupree."

"Oh, really," said Pastor Matthew. "Why were they there?"

"They came to evict me from my house," Louella said.

"What? Why?" Pastor Matthew asked.

"Mr. James Dupree now owns my house," Louella said.

"I don't understand," Pastor Matthew answered. "I thought you own your home."

"So did I," Louella said. "But Mr. Dupree was able to pull some strings with the county office. He seems to have a handle on the entire city of Rockville. He got them to transfer the title of my house to him."

Pastor Matthew was horrified. "Unbelievable," he said. "I've seen on TV specific warnings about protecting your title against such kinds of transfers. Who would've thought it would happen right here in Rockville?" Pastor Matthew asked Louella to give him permission to turn on the speaker on his phone so his wife, Sharon, could join the conversation.

"Of course, go ahead and put your phone on speaker, but," Louella went on, "I find it unbelievable that someone can be so greedy as to take my home away from me," Louella said. "And I think I know why Mr. Dupree is doing this."

"Why would he do that?" Pastor Matthew inquired.

"Yeah, why would he do that?" Sharon wondered as well.

"He seems to be retaliating against me for rejecting his offer to join his company as one of his directors," Louella answered. "I understand from different people that no one says no to Mr. Dupree. But I said no to him because I wanted to continue working on my flower business. . . Oh my God!" Louella gasped. "Could he be behind the vandalism on my shop?" Her eyes opened wide in terror when that realization hit her.

"Hold on, Louella," Pastor Matthew said. "You're going too fast."

"I'm sorry, Pastor," said Louella. "But it all makes sense now: The message from the brown envelope seemed to indicate Mr. Dupree was behind the vandalism in my shop. My shop is gone and my home is about to go. They all seem to point to one person, and Detective Rick Mulley is dead because he was beginning to zero-in on Mr. Dupree. That's why Jason had to leave the service abruptly."

Louella seemed hysterical. Pastor Matthew began to see the sense of what she was saying. "Louella, calm down a minute here. You seem to be on to something. This is a very dangerous thing wrapping itself around you, and I seem to be walking into it as well."

"I was just calling you for some spiritual strength," she said. "Would you kindly pray for me right now, for my safety, and for all this—that the truth would come to light?"

"Absolutely," said Pastor Matthew. "Let's pray." At one end of the line, Pastor Matthew and his wife, Sharon, went down on their knees as Louella, at the other end of the line, lifted her right hand to the heavens, beseeching God to intervene in their situation. Pastor Matthew prayed as passionately as if he was praying for himself except that he was praying for one of his congregation members. With intermittent interjections of "Amen" and "Yes" from Sharon, Pastor Matthew prayed for Louella's protection and for a quick resolution to the enormous problems Louella seemed to be facing. Louella drew strength from the fact that her own pastor was truly concerned about her needs. When the prayer was over, they all said, "Amen," in a chorus, and they felt as if the angels had joined them in that brief teleconference prayer service.

29

MEANWHILE, SAM CALLED MR. Dupree to inquire about what Louella had shared with him. "Is it true," he asked, "that you have taken ownership of Louella's home?"

"You're right," Mr. Dupree said. "It's now my property."

"How in the world were you able to pull that off?" Sam asked.

"I have my ways and means," Mr. Dupree said.

"But why would you forcefully take a home owned by a hardworking citizen away from her?" Sam asked. "You know how hard she's worked to establish herself."

"No one outranks me in this city, and certainly not a woman of her kind," Mr. Dupree said.

"Uncle!' Sam half shouted and half rebuked him. "Stop this! Just stop this! This is way beneath you."

"Oh, yeah!" scoffed Mr. Dupree. "And who are you to tell me that?"

"You're supposed to be my uncle, remember? And Louella and I are beginning to hit it off quite well."

"Really! I didn't know you were developing a relationship with Louella," Mr. Dupree said. "I thought Nancy was your girl."

"Nancy is a nice and pretty girl," Sam said. "But I'm drawn to Louella more because she's a principled, godly woman."

"Ah, you're beginning to get all preachy with me," Mr. Dupree chided. "Are you seriously pursuing a relationship with Louella?"

"Yes, Mr. Dupree, and you're ruining it. Remember, I introduced you to her as my uncle."

"Well, for starters," Mr. Dupree said, "You lied to her. I'm not your uncle."

"You really are my uncle," Sam said. "You're my dad's stepbrother. You may not have been related to him by blood, but you're my uncle."

"Fine, fine, fine," responded Mr. Dupree. "But understand that I can't go back on my decision to evict Louella from that home. She said no to my proposal. No one says no to me, not now, not ever!"

"Seriously?"

"Seriously."

"Are you not going to bend your rules just this once for me?" Sam asked, almost pleading.

"Why are you so much into this girl?" asked Mr. Dupree, somewhat surprised at Sam's insistence.

"Because I'm interested in having a meaningful relationship with her," said Sam. "I'm very serious about this. I'm even hoping that at some point I'll propose to her if everything goes well. This is a person that could be your niece, uncle."

"Okay," Mr. Dupree seemed to relax his stance. "How about I meet you halfway? For now, I'll not evict Louella from her house,. . . er,. . . my house. I'll even go as far as funding the reconstruction of her flower shop and making it as good as new. But since she'll be joining the Dupree family, she might as well consider, very seriously, the offer to join Dupree Enterprises. Let her know that."

"You can't be serious," Sam said. "You want her to reconsider the stance she took with regard to your earlier proposal?"

"You heard me right," Dupree said.

"How do you even know that she'll put all her heart into it if she takes you up on that offer?"

"She has no option but to put all her heart into it," said Mr. Dupree. "Otherwise, the deal is off the table."

"Listen," Sam went on, "I need to take a more positive message to Louella than that. You can't deny that she's a principled, industrious, and, by all counts, beautiful woman. I'm interested in taking care of her and pursuing a serious relationship with her. Please, reconsider some of your demands. Give her back her home but don't demand that she join Dupree Enterprises. That would be a serious overreach. Let her make that decision herself. Think about it, if she decides to join Dupree Enterprises without your manipulation, you'll feel good about it because it'll be a genuine and honest move from her heart."

"Give me time to think about your counteroffer," said Mr. Dupree. Just know that I'm absolutely ticked off by her refusal to accept my proposal. I could have made a lot of money by establishing a business at the exact location of her flower shop."

The last comment by Mr. Dupree didn't go unnoticed by Sam, and he wanted to inquire about it, so he decided to fire his question.

"Please tell me, sir, that you had nothing to do with the vandalism of that flower shop."

"Ask me no questions and I'll tell you no lies," Mr. Dupree responded.

"Mr. Dupree, I want to ask you again," Sam pressed. "Please tell me that the vandalism on Louella's flower shop wasn't orchestrated by you."

"This conversation is over," said Mr. Dupree. "I'll get back to you on your counteroffer."

As Sam prepared to make his next statement, the phone went silent. Mr. Dupree's last words made him very uncomfortable. When he had asked Mason Kruger about the vandalism, Mason challenged him to fill in the pieces of the puzzle himself. He wondered if Mr. Dupree was really a piece to that puzzle. Furthermore, Sam wasn't sure he had gained much ground in his conversation with Mr. Dupree, his uncle, or step uncle. But at least Mr. Dupree had backed out of evicting Louella from her home. It sounded rather strange and profoundly wrong to Sam's ears that Louella was getting evicted from a home she rightfully owned just because some business tycoon in town manipulated the powers-that-be to transfer the title of her home from Louella to himself. It felt even more uncomfortable that Sam related to that tycoon as his uncle.

30

Louella knew she was in trouble—deep trouble. But she also sensed danger—great danger. If she didn't own the home, as the evidence clearly suggested, then her stay in that home was only a matter of weeks. She felt as if heart failure was coming her way, but something about Pastor Matthew's prayer gave her strength. The evening was approaching fast. The day's events were too many for her. She was surprised they all fitted into her Sunday afternoon. As she tried to make sense of what she'd just lived through, her phone rang again. It was Sam.

"Hello, Sam," she said as he picked up the phone.

"Hi, Louella," Sam replied. "I talked with my uncle. He's very adamant and doesn't want to give up ownership of the home."

"Sam," Louella almost yelled at him. "This is NOT Mr. Dupree's home. He's taking it illegally from me. It's daylight robbery!"

"I know, Louella. I know," Sam answered. "But get this. I managed to convince him to stop evicting you from your own home."

"Oh, you did," Louella said.

Sam thought he noticed a sense of relief in Louella's voice. "As a matter of fact, I did," he said. "But he insists on having you come on board with Dupree Enterprises. He also wants to underwrite the cost of rebuilding your flower shop."

"What's wrong with your uncle?" Louella asked. "My shop was fully insured. Insurance will take care of everything."

"I'd forgotten about that part of the story," Sam said. "I even forgot to bring it to my uncle's attention. But he's choosing not to make good his threat to evict you."

"I hate to admit that I am relieved," said Louella. "But thank you for your intervention."

"You're welcome," Sam said. "But my uncle did have another demand."

"What is it?"

"He wants you to accept his proposal to join Dupree Enterprises unconditionally. I have to tell you, though, that I pushed back on that."

"Listen, Sam," Louella said, "I have no interest in pursuing a business partnership with a person who's causing me so much pain. It won't be a workable partnership at all."

"I understand," Sam answered. "But like I told you, I pushed back on that request."

"So, what did he say when you pushed back?" Louella asked.

"He promised to get back to me on that," Sam replied. "He needed time to think about it."

"Sam, I don't trust your uncle one bit. I'm sorry to say that," Louella answered, and went on. "Who in their right mind would join ranks with a person seeking to destroy their livelihood at every corner? Would you?"

"No, I wouldn't," Sam consented and added, "I'm ashamed to call him my uncle. I hope, though, you can rest assured he won't evict you from your own home."

"Sam, like I said, I don't trust your uncle. He seems to speak from both sides of his mouth," Louella observed.

"There are some things about him that I don't know," Sam continued. "He takes me by surprise at every turn. I just don't understand how he became a member of the Dupree family. But I can assure you that if he reneges on his promise not to evict you, I'll do everything within my power to fight it and to cut ties with him forever."

"Thank you, Sam," Louella said and hung up the phone. That promise from Sam sounded distantly reassuring to Louella. At least she had one more person willing to come to her side, besides the pastor, Sharon, and Julie. For a while she had felt all alone. Her mother wasn't there to help her. The pastor and his family were the only family she knew. To have Sam promise to come to her side was somewhat reassuring.

Louella remembered that she had brought the thumb drive with her after they viewed its contents at the pastor's office. She wanted to take a closer look at the documents one more time. They were all so dumbfounded by its contents that they didn't give those documents a second look. Since Mr. Dupree had been implicated in the documents, she wanted to see if anything in the documents further suggested that he was responsible for the attack on her flower shop. In light of the fact that he wanted her evicted from her own home, it wasn't too farfetched for her to believe Mr. Dupree was behind her woes. As she turned on her computer, her phone rang again. It was Jason.

"Jason!" Louella shouted his name across the room. "Where are you?"

"Hi, Louella," Jason answered. "Is someone with you?"

"No. I'm alone at my house," she said. "I came home from church only to find some members of Rockville Police Department here with a man by the name of James Dupree. They were coming here to evict me from my house."

"Louella," Jason replied, "have you taken a look at the contents of the envelope?"

"Yes, I have," Louella said, "and I did see Mr. Dupree's name in quite a number of the conversations."

"Louella," Jason went on, "be very careful about Mr. Dupree. Did you see the one part of the document implicating Mr. Dupree in the vandalization of your flower shop?"

"I hadn't gone that far," Louella gasped. "Is that information in the thumb drive?"

"My brother was beginning to zero-in on Mr. Dupree, and because of the influence Mr. Dupree seems to have on Chief Drake Riley, they made sure they took care of him in some way."

"But where are you, Jason?" Louella asked.

"As soon as I stepped out of the church building, two officers started chasing me in their car. and I decided they weren't going to get me."

"Oh! What did you do?"

"I drove off at top speed, and when I got onto the freeway, I was determined to beat them in the chase. Unfortunately, as I approached a bend, I was going too fast, lost control of the truck. and flipped as I negotiated the bend. The truck soared into the air and went over the cliff, crashing almost forty feet below. It became a mangled wreck. Apparently, they didn't come to see if I was okay. I think they assumed I was dead. I don't know how long I was there because I was stunned by the impact. But when I came to, I crawled out of the car and I could hear sirens blaring in the distance. I figured they came to look for me, so I took off."

"Could you not wait for the paramedics to get to you?"

"At this point in the game," Jason replied, "I don't know who's for me or who's against me. We have quite a few rotten apples in the city of Rockville.

But you take a look at those documents. Mr. Dupree is certainly involved in the vandalism of your shop."

Louella was absolutely furious. Her suspicions were confirmed. She remembered how Mason came to see her at Rockville Regional Hospital. Was he pretending to help her? He even went as far as assessing the damage at her flower shop. Wait a minute, Sam was there too? Did Sam know about the attack on her business? She immediately called Sam back.

"Hello, Louella," Sam answered the phone.

"Sam," Louella asked. "Are you aware that your uncle was behind the vandalism at my flower shop?"

"I suspected the same, and I still do suspect that," Sam said. "But I really have no proof. And if it is true, I'll spare no effort in ensuring he's brought to justice." Sam sounded genuinely emphatic.

"What led you to suspect that?" Louella asked.

Sam answered, "My conversation with Mason Kruger shortly after visiting your flower shop was quite revealing. He didn't come clean when I challenged him about it. Moreover, he told me he would leave it to me to fill in the pieces of the puzzle."

"Well," Louella answered, "I think your uncle is involved. And if I find tangible proof that he is, I'll let you know."

Louella wasn't sure she'd let Sam know anyway. It was her way of ending the conversation, but she was now more determined than ever to peruse the documents in the BS envelope. She had wondered why it was titled BS. It seemed to be a decoy until she discovered, much later, from Jason, that BS stood for Bombshell. The light dawned on her. The information she had in her hand would make the difference between her survival and her going down. It would rattle the city of Rockville to its core if that information came out. She was determined to get it out. She was determined to take it to Action News and let it air on Primetime for the whole world to see.

She took the time to read through the documents thoroughly. What she saw revolted her as profoundly as it frightened her. She was a major target of Mr. Dupree. Mr. Dupree was behind the vandalism in her shop. The evidence was undeniable. Mr. Dupree was behind Detective Rick Mulley's death. Mr. Dupree was behind the fraudulent transfer of her title from her name to Dupree Enterprises. All that information was contained in the thumb drive, and the reason Detective Rick Mulley was dead is because he had unearthed a major scandal that would end the careers of Drake Riley and Dupree Enterprises. That explained why she was a target. It further explained why Jason Mulley wanted to see her. It all came together. Louella Goodman was trembling like a poplar tree.

31

Louella decided to waste no more time. The funeral service would be happening in less than seventy-two hours. Jason needed to be at his brother's funeral, but he couldn't do it while on the run from the police. Just as importantly, Louella had to stop Mr. Dupree's insatiable desire for dominance and wealth. Her best recourse would be to head off to the news station at Action News and hand over the contents of that envelope to the reporters. But she was unsure of one thing: Would that station report the story faithfully? Perhaps Action News should have custody of that information, but perhaps someone else needs a copy of that thumb drive besides Action News. She began listing possible additional custodians.

After making sure she made an extra copy of the thumb drive's contents onto another thumb drive, she picked up her car keys, opened her garage door and stepped into the car. As she pulled out of the garage, she noticed a squad car parked about fifty yards from her home. Under normal circumstances, she wouldn't have paid much attention to it, but the circumstances, on this Sunday evening, weren't normal, at least not for her. She took a closer look at that police car and noticed that the officer was one among those who attended service at Rockville Community Church earlier that day. Are they keeping an eye on her? Maybe they were. But then again, maybe they weren't.

She decided to ignore it and kept going. As she turned into the highway to begin her drive, she could see from her rearview mirror that the police car also started following her. The officer was keeping his distance, neither coming too close nor staying out of sight. Jason's story began to haunt her. Jason had asked her to surrender the contents of that thumb drive to the local news station, and she was determined to do just that. Once she got onto the freeway, she did everything she could to give the police behind her no specific reason to stop her. She observed the speed limit. She wondered what she needed to do to stop him from following her, so she pretended to go toward her vandalized flower shop. She took the exit from the freeway that led to the flower shop. She even went as far as parking her car at her usual parking spot whenever she reported to work.

She stepped out of her car and pretended to inspect the progress made on the flower shop, which was almost nil. The do-not-cross police tape was still in place because it was still an active crime scene. Because of the information she now had, she knew that not much would come through in terms of the investigation. The investigators were Mr. Dupree's puppets. She looked behind her to see if the officer was still following her. He seemed to have driven off when it became clear to him that Louella was merely heading to her shop. Thankfully, her shop had a backdoor. If that policeman was still there, she would use the backdoor and slip unnoticed to Action News station, which was three blocks away from her shop. She took one more look to see if he had really gone. To her surprise, the cop had merely driven past her and returned to park not too far from her car, perhaps thirty yards away. Clearly, they were making a statement, perhaps even instilling fear in her to keep her from trying anything silly. They were watching. But then she remembered she couldn't get into her shop. It was an active crime scene, and she wasn't allowed to cross into the premises.

She decided to walk toward a nearby bakery. She stepped inside and found a table. She wasn't particularly interested in eating anything, but she needed to give her stalker the idea that she was out to eat. The officer was nowhere to be seen. She looked again and couldn't find him, so she slowly walked toward the station. When she got to the front desk, she needed to have some security clearance.

"Can I help you, ma'am?" the person at the front desk inquired.

"Is it possible for me to talk to a reporter about a pressing matter?" Louella asked.

"Sure," the person at the front desk said. "Just wait here and someone will come to you. But I need to get your details first." She got Louella's name, number, and street address and noted the purpose of her visit. The lady then dialed a number and appeared to talk to someone in the building. She hung up the phone and said, "Someone will be right with you."

"Thank you very much," Louella said. Before too long, a smartly dressed lady, whom Louella was sure she had seen on TV, appeared.

"You must be Louella," the news anchor said. "My name is Gloria Steele. I'm a news anchor with Action News."

"I know you," Louella said. "I see you on TV almost every day. So nice to see you in person."

"Thank you, Louella," she said. "Please come with me." Louella followed her into something that looked like a studio. The cameras were not running though the place was a beehive of activity.

"Please have a seat here," she said, pointing to a comfortable office chair next to hers.

"Thank you," Louella said.

"How can I help you?" Gloria Steele asked.

"I have some information that you might find very newsworthy," Louella said. And she began to tell her story. The more she talked, the wider Gloria Steele's mouth got. She began with the vandalism in her office, which Gloria remembered covering. She talked about Detective Rick Mulley's death, and she noticed that Gloria's eyes almost popped out of their sockets. She mentioned how the police came to her church and tried to arrest her for being in possession of some privileged information. Gloria appeared thunderstruck.

"And to prove everything I've shared with you," Louella said, "I have all the documentation in this thumb drive. If you look into it, you'll find all the details in there."

Gloria was elated. She jumped at the opportunity of handling a news item that would keep their viewers glued to their television sets. She looked through the documents, and all of them confirmed Louella's report.

"Moreover," Louella said, "Detective Rick Mulley's funeral will be at Rockville Community Church on Wednesday. Jason, his brother, can't attend the funeral because he's running away from the police."

The entire conversation left Gloria Steele visibly stunned. Louella wasn't sure she'd seen any reporter, let alone Gloria, so stunned by what she shared with the news station. In a certain sense, she felt really uncomfortable about dragging her church into this scandal, even though nothing in the scandal characterized Rockville Community Church negatively. It just happened to be caught in the crossfire between officers and certain members, herself included. She desperately hoped her pastor would be okay with this trend of events. What she wasn't sure about, however, is whether she could trust Gloria to report this story without manipulation from Rockville Police Department or from Mr. Dupree. These two entities seemed to have an upper hand in every area of Rockville. Thankfully she had made another copy of the thumb drive, but she was unsure where she would send it at this point.

32

As Louella stepped out of Action News studios, a phrase she'd heard before popped into her mind: Mission accomplished. She believed she'd done what Jason had pleaded with her to do. As she went past the reception desk, she thanked the lady for helping her see Gloria Steele who was following closely behind. Gloria thanked her for coming, shook her hand, and encouraged her to stand by for the news item to feature the following day. Exactly when that would happen, she couldn't tell, but it would likely hit the 7 am news.

Louella was grateful to the staff of Action News. It was always affirming and assuring to her when any news organization was on her side. She couldn't imagine what it would feel like for such a reputable organization to be doing a story casting her in bad light. As she stepped out of the premises, she remembered she was still under surveillance by someone from Rockville Police Department. She looked right, left, upward and forward to see if anyone was watching her. She then walked down the three blocks to find her car. It was still there just as she had left it. She looked in the direction of where she last saw the policeman. He was gone. *Maybe he got bored and gave up looking for me,* Louella thought. She was wrong.

The cop had merely changed his vantage point and was parked at a different intersection. As Louella started heading back home, the officer slowly pulled out of his parking spot and began trailing her again, not too closely and not too far either. *Holy moly! These guys never give up*, she complained to herself. She wondered if she would draw too much attention to herself if she called Pastor Matthew to let him know what she'd been up to. But she was afraid that the cop would pull her over for distracted driving. That thought caused her to hold off on that idea and decided to wait until she got home. *Perhaps, then, I could call Jason*, she wondered.

Then she remembered it still amounted to the same fear. *This is slavery,* she thought. *I don't feel free to do what I would do under normal circumstances.* She looked through her rearview mirror and noticed the cop still trailing her. She wondered if he was aware of the fact that she had given the city's major news station some profoundly damning report about them. If it came out as Gloria promised it would, the news story would be huge. She was still very scared of the possible implications. What if Gloria is on the city's side? What if she was Mr. Dupree's puppet? She couldn't rule that out. She was taking a big risk by handing over that information to Action News. As she thought through the implications, she consoled herself with the fact that she still had a copy of the evidence, which she could present elsewhere. Exactly where, she still hadn't figured out.

As these thoughts ran through her mind, she found herself pulling into her driveway and into the garage. It was one of those drives where she never paid attention to where she was headed because her thoughts took her captive. She couldn't remember taking all the correct exits and the right and left turns and observing the stop signs. She guessed she had been so used to making that drive to and from work that obeying those signs became second nature to her. Sunday, 9 pm was approaching fast. Her time at the news station was worth it. She got out of her car and began dialing Pastor Matthew's number for the update. She could hear Pastor Matthew picking up the phone at the other end of the line.

"This is Matthew," he said.

"Hello, Pastor," Louella responded. "I'm sorry for calling you this late. Do you have a minute?"

"Yes, Louella," Pastor Matthew replied. "What's up?"

"I decided to honor Jason's request to take the thumb drive to Action News."

"You did?" Pastor Matthew seemed surprised, not because she did it but because of how soon she did it.

"Yes, sir," she said. "I just got back from an interview with Gloria Steele, the news anchor."

"Yeah. She's on every morning," Pastor Matthew said. "I suppose you told them everything, including the funeral service on Wednesday, correct?"

"As a matter of fact, I did," Louella said. "But they now know how James Dupree orchestrated the entire operation of the vandalism at my shop and who the thugs were."

"Dear Lord Jesus Christ," Pastor Matthew said. "Was all that information on the thumb drive?"

"Yes, Pastor. What Sharon, you, and I saw was only a fraction of the document." Louella went on. "What portion of the story they plan to run, I can't tell. I'm crossing my fingers and expecting a bombshell. You remember that's what the BS on the brown envelope stood for."

"I do remember," Pastor Matthew said. "I have to tell you, when I saw those initials, I wondered why anyone would bring an envelope with those letters to church. My mind went somewhere else."

"I know, right?" Louella said. "It seemed quite an appropriate decoy under the circumstances."

"So what's next?" Pastor Matthew asked.

"We can only wait and see what happens," Louella responded.

"Well, you have a restful night," Pastor Matthew said. "It's been a long, tiring day for you. I don't mind being in the news for the right reasons. I hope Action News won't cast us in bad light. The devil is a liar, you know?"

"I know, Pastor," Louella continued.

"Listen," Pastor Matthew went on, "Don't forget to pray. The Lord acts when we seek him in prayer. Prayer has always been my weapon. I urge you to lift everything that has transpired today before the Lord in prayer."

"You got it. I'll do so before going to bed tonight. I still want to call Jason and tell him the work has been done."

"You do that," Pastor Matthew said. "See you on Wednesday at the funeral."

They both hung up the phone and, immediately, Louella began dialing Jason Mulley. She wanted him to know, as soon as possible, that she had handed over the document to Action News. She was excited to tell him the news but wasn't sure if Jason would pick up the phone immediately. He picked it up.

"This is Jason," she heard him say.

"Jason," Louella said, "Misson accomplished! The thumb drive is with Action News just as you had asked me to do."

"I know," Jason said. "Gloria Steele called me and was asking me to verify the information you gave her. She is absolutely on top of things and wants the whole story to air tomorrow at 7 am. But she wants to meet me in person, and I don't know where I can meet her safely."

Louella's heart skipped a beat . . . literally. "She called you? Oh my word!"

"Yes, she did," Jason said. "Thank you for handing that information to her."

"So when and where do you plan to meet her?" Louella asked.

"I really don't know. I can't go to my house right now. It's under twenty-four-hour surveillance by the Rockville Police Department. They're looking for me all over the place."

"So where are you right now?" Louella asked.

"That's something I can't tell you. I don't know if my phone is bugged or not." Jason replied.

Louella hadn't thought about her phone being bugged. What if they heard all her conversations with Pastor Matthew and now with Jason? Real fear gripped her. Could that be the reason they were watching her every move? Louella got really worried.

"Jason," Louella said, "please be careful."

"I will be," he answered. "It's not lost on me that if they got my brother killed, I could be next. That isn't beyond the realm of possibilities."

"Don't you think they believe you died in the wreck?" Louella asked.

"Perhaps. But why are they putting my home under twenty-four-hour surveillance?" he queried.

"Perhaps they want to know who else is connected to you," Louella replied.

"That may be the case," Jason said. "But I'm not about to take risks to find out why they're there."

"Good point," Louella noted. "Hey, listen. Do you think you'll be at the funeral on Wednesday?"

"No. It's too dangerous," he replied. "Moreover, it's a funeral organized by the Rockville Police Department. I don't want any part of it. If things settle, as I now hope they will, I'll ask Pastor Matthew to hold a more heart-felt service for my brother."

"You know, that's a really good idea. The key phrase is *if things settle*," Louella said.

They ended their conversation. Louella went down on her knees beside her bed and prayed furiously. She prayed for Pastor Matthew. She prayed for Jason. She prayed for Sam. She also prayed for Mr. Dupree. Each prayer item was different. She prayed for protection for Pastor Matthew and for Jason. She prayed for discernment for Sam. And she prayed for Mr. Dupree's salvation. She got up from her bedside, picked up her Bible, and read Psalm 23. She read it over and over again. She even prayed through it. Then she went back on her knees and prayed for Wednesday's funeral service. She asked the Lord to deploy his angelic hosts to Rockville Community Church at precisely the time of the funeral. When she completed her little one-woman prayer service, she got up and felt something she had never felt before. Something assured her that her words had reached the Lord's ear, and that God was responding to her request. Perhaps this was why she went through everything she'd gone through—to draw closer to the Lord, much closer than she'd ever felt. It gave her a sense of victory. Not even the successful business sales that she'd had before the vandalism could match this sense of satisfaction. It gave her a new sense of purpose. Could it be that the Lord used all these events to bring her to this very point? Was that a price too high to pay for God to get her attention? It seemed to her that the Lord allowed it to happen and used it for this very purpose. She read somewhere in the book of Genesis that what Joseph's brothers meant for evil, God meant for good.

33

Jason was concerned for his own safety. He was sitting in one of the bedrooms in his fiancée's parents' house. He wasn't sure what the safest place in Rockville would be. He knew that not every police officer in Rockville was involved in the scandal of his brother's death. What he didn't know, however, is who the clean police officers were. Under the circumstances, it was very difficult for him to know the answer to this question. He thought long and hard about what he needed to do. What if he hadn't succeeded in handing over the brown envelope to Louella? Who else would he entrust with such valuable information? But what if Action News folks were in on this. Where else would he go? All these questions swirled in his mind, driving him insane.

As he looked at all the different scenarios and possibilities, one thought came to mind: the FBI. Perhaps he should have entrusted the thumb drive to the FBI. He decided to give the FBI a try. He looked up the local listings for any FBI office closest to his house. It turned out that the closest office was about one hour away. He had no car, and he wasn't sure how he could get there. As he was thinking about this, Sally walked into the room.

"So," she started. "What are you thinking?"

"All the information you saw is in the hands of Action News," he said, "but I'm not sure they will take action on what we've given them. Even if they could take action, what would it be?"

She asked again, "What are you thinking of doing, then?"

"I'm thinking," Jason said, "that my surest bet for bringing my brother's killers to justice is to contact the FBI."

"Really?" she asked. "And how will you go about doing that?"

"Well," he said, "they do have a website that lists the street address of the office nearest to us."

"You want to go there when the cops are looking for you all over Rockville?" she asked.

"Exactly," he responded. "It's our best chance of having this case solved. My only alternative is to remain a fugitive for the foreseeable future with no end in sight."

"You're right about that," Sally said. "Perhaps I can drive you there. When do you want to go? After the funeral, possibly?"

"No," Jason said. "I want to go now!"

"Now?" Sally gasped. "Are you crazy?"

"Right now, everyone connected to this case is crazy," Jason said. "I might as well live up to that expectation. Desperate times call for desperate measures."

"Oh dear," she said. "Are you ready to go now, then?"

"If you're ready to take me, I'm ready to go," he said.

Sally went downstairs to tell her parents that she was taking her soon-to-be husband to the FBI office in Lockridge, a much bigger city than Rockville. Her parents expressed their concerns, but they saw the sense in making this move in light of what Jason and Sally had shared with them, so Jason and Sally jumped into her Ford Taurus and headed for Lockridge. Every time Jason saw a police car, his paranoia got the better of him. He didn't really have to worry about that. For the most part, the cops thought he had been incapacitated by the accident in some way, even if he might not have died in it. The paramedics at the scene of his accident had reported that the driver of the truck was missing. That explained why so many officers were hibernating by his home.

As they drove along the back roads toward Lockridge, driving in the dark made it especially challenging. But they soldiered on. It took them close to eighty minutes to get to Lockridge. Both Jason and Sally were tired. It was a long drive for them. Indeed, it had been a long day for Jason. Who goes back onto the road after watching his car flip dangerously into the air several times and land down a cliff forty feet below? Jason was right. Only a crazy person would venture out in this way. As they got closer to Lockridge, the skyscrapers began to emerge. The differently colored neon lights seem to invite them to the town that, by and large, seemed to have tapered off in activity, given that it was a Sunday night. The GPS brought them squarely into the heart of town. Once they reached their destination, they heard the ever-assuring voice from the device: "You have arrived."

Jason wasn't sure what kind of reception he'd get. Moreover, the security in the federal building was tight. No one really walks into any FBI office without making an appointment unless, of course, the person was under arrest. But Jason and Sally thought they'd give it a chance. After they drove into the parking garage of the federal building and parked their Taurus, Sally had an idea.

"Jason," she started, "I suspect entering this federal building would be a little bit of a challenge without some kind of appointment. How about we call them first and let them know we have some important information that we think they need to hear. That might give us a chance to talk to someone."

"You know," Jason said. "That's a great idea. Can you find the number on their website?"

Sally browsed through the website and finally located the phone number. She dialed the number, and someone picked up. Sally started talking first. She introduced herself and made it known that they were outside the building and that they had some very important information they needed to pass on to them. As they kept talking back and forth, the person at the other end of the line asked to speak with Jason. Jason introduced himself and explained to them what had happened the past couple of days from Thursday that week until that Sunday. They eventually understood that Jason was the brother of the deceased cop, Rick Mulley. They learned that he had all the documents to prove what he was saying and that they had passed on a copy of that information to Action News in nearby Rockville.

After about a 30-minute conversation, two members of the FBI came out of the building and into the parking garage. The federal agents spotted them and walked toward them. The grilling was rigorous, but they established the consistency of Jason's report and the sincerity of his presentation. After seeing beyond reasonable doubt that Jason was telling the truth, Jason handed them a copy of a thumb drive that he had made containing all the information he had talked about. They put it in a Ziplock bag and went through the details one more time. One of them walked back into the building with the bag. After about 25 minutes, the agent walked back outside.

Finally, one of the federal agents said, "We're aware of what's been going on in Rockville. The story you tell us is consistent with what we know. Come on inside. There's someone we think you need to meet."

Jason was sure he was going to meet face-to-face with the Agent in Charge. His heart began to pound. Will he have to repeat his story? That possibility got him concerned, but he steadied his walk as Sally locked her hand into his. If ever Jason needed her most at any stage in his life, this was it. She was ready to stand by her man. As they walked through the security checkpoint, they found themselves being led into an interrogation room.

Great, Jason thought, *another round of interrogations coming our way!* The agents invited them to have a seat. One of them sat there with them while the other agent asked them to wait as she got the person the agents wanted them to meet. The federal agent that sat with them continued making his inquiries, clarifying Jason's and Sally's comments. Jason was beginning to wish the entire exercise would end soon.

As they were sitting there still talking, they heard a knock on the door. The agent who had stepped out was stepping back in with a familiar face right behind her—a face Jason knew only too well: Rick Mulley, his brother! Sally gasped as if she had seen a ghost—her mouth wide open and the tips of three of her fingers touching her upper lip.

"RRRIIICK!" Jason screamed, jumped, and hugged his brother tighter than he had ever hugged anyone else in his life, almost wrestling him to the floor. "You're supposed to be . . ."

"Dead?" Rick finished the sentence, transforming it into a question. "I almost died, but I'm alive."

"Rick! Boy, am I so glad to see you!" Jason screamed at the top of his lungs. He cried, and hugged Rick again, and sobbed, and wailed, and hugged his brother again.

"Your funeral is on Wednesday, my brother!" Jason said. "Will you be attending your funeral? I know this sounds crazy, but why aren't you dead?"

"It's a long story," Rick said. "I was getting closer and closer to cracking the case involving Rockville's Finest Flowers, but in the process, I unearthed some very sensitive information. I stepped on some toes, and somebody wanted me dead. I guess someone knew I made a frequent stop at *Stay Sober*. They knew my routine so when I asked for some wine, someone in the kitchen laced that shot with potassium cyanide, minimal enough to go unnoticed in my glass, and I think it was supposed to be lethal enough to kill me. Whatever amount they put in that glass wasn't enough to kill me. The doctors at Rockville Regional suspected foul play. One of the doctors there happens to be a brother of one of the agents here, and I understand from his brother that the surgeon knows me. In fact, I believe I know that surgeon. The doctor immediately transferred me to Lockridge Memorial Hospital and, for my protection and theirs, sent a false report to the

Rockville Police Department saying I had succumbed to the poison. Chief Riley believed him and began planning my funeral without bothering to confirm my death, and that's how he got in touch with you."

Jason said, "That explains why my repeated attempts to come and view your body at the morgue kept falling on deaf ears! I was supposed to see your dead body today. Am I glad I'm seeing you alive!" he exclaimed, jumping up and down repeatedly like a teenager. "So," he went on, "what do we do about Wednesday? I was so concerned I'd miss your funeral because, as you know, I'm a fugitive. I passed on everything you left behind in your BS envelope to Action News. The guys in this office also have the same information. And by the way," Jason went on, "this whole story is supposed to feature at 7 am tomorrow, so you might need to turn the TV on and watch the events unfold."

Rick said, "I can assure you, Wednesday will be a very interesting day. I want to be there for my own funeral. It'll give me an idea of how the disciples of Jesus reacted when they saw him resurrected! It's interesting how that passage of Scripture is coming alive before our very own eyes. This experience is putting a different spin to my understanding of that story!"

As they were talking to each other, the federal agents had slipped out. Rick knew what they were planning to do. They were working on a strategy to arrest the two hit men—Hank and Larry. They were also planning to arrest Chief Drake Riley, Mr. Dupree, and Mason Kruger. The one place they knew all three would be together would be at Rick's funeral. It had been posted as a celebration of life. It was gearing itself up to be a celebration like no other!

34

Before Jason and Sally left the FBI office in Lockridge, they wondered what to do about Rick's funeral on Wednesday.

"Rick," Jason said, "Do you really want to go to your funeral?" That question sounded rather strange to all of them, but it had to be asked.

"Well," Rick responded, "If those people wanted me dead a few days ago, they'll still want me dead on Wednesday."

"That shouldn't be a problem," said one of the FBI agents, listening to the conversation.

"What? Me being dead would be no problem?" Rick asked.

"No, not that. Not having to worry about the aftermath of you showing up," he said.

"And why wouldn't that be a problem?" Rick asked.

"I'm sure we'll be there to arrest the rogue police officers," the agent said.

"The FBI is attending the funeral service?" Jason asked.

"Yes. We have an elaborate plan in place. It's a funeral service for a fallen police officer, so we imagine a lot of your colleagues will be there," the FBI agent said, looking directly at Rick.

"I'm beginning to feel really good about attending my own funeral," Rick said. "This should be something special."

"But how, exactly, should we go about this?" Jason asked.

"The first thing we need to do is to figure out how we can get an empty casket to the church," Rick said, "which shouldn't be difficult. Even though Drake Riley is a bad apple, we have a mutual friend at the funeral home. We can ask him to take an empty casket to church for us. He's a close friend of mine and knows Riley isn't a principled man. From what I suspect, my friend must be grieving over my death. I'm sure he'll be extremely delighted to know I'm still around."

"But wait," Jason said. "Won't he let the cat out of the bag that you're still alive?"

"I trust him," Rick said. "I have no doubt he'll be tight-lipped about me being alive."

"But how do we reach out to him?" Jason kept prodding.

"Leave that to me," said the FBI agent. "Give me the name of the funeral director, and we'll take it from there. All we'll need to tell him is to have a casket ready, and he'll tell officer Riley that Rick's family will take care of the casket. Chief Riley won't suspect that Rick is still alive. In fact, he'll want Rick's family to be there to give him an idea of Jason's whereabouts, assuming Jason himself chooses not to attend the service. Meanwhile, if you believe he's as reliable as you say he is, Rick, we can arrange for him to meet you before the funeral so you can tell him why he needs to take an empty casket to church! Jason, will you be at the funeral?"

"Oh, you can be sure I'll be there," Jason said with great determination. "I wouldn't miss the fun for anything."

"If you'll excuse me, then," the agent said, "let me get the process going. I think we have an interesting funeral coming up very soon. Friends, it's been wonderful to work with you."

"How do you plan to get to Rockville, Rick?" Jason asked. "I cannot have you in my home because it is surrounded by Riley's boys."

"I still feel weak from the poisoning," Rick said, "But since the funeral is only three days away, I think I should come with you, assuming Sally doesn't mind."

"I'd be honored to have a living dead man in my car!" Sally said.

After making sure everyone concerned with Rick's case at the FBI knew about his ride to Rockville, Rick decided to travel with Jason and Sally. Since most of this was taking place early Monday morning, while it was still dark, none of them had gotten much sleep. Sally, however, was used to working night shifts, so she had little difficulty driving her Taurus back to Rockville. Having spoken with the FBI agents, and since he knew what was brewing, Jason was braver than he had been earlier that day. He gained confidence from the fact that he wasn't seen as the bad guy. He encouraged Sally to use the freeway back to Rockville.

"That doesn't mean you should be careless, though," Jason said.

"I'm not a careless driver," Sally said, somewhat irritated. "Who among us just had a wreck?" she asked sarcastically.

"I was being chased by the police, for crying out loud," Jason fought back.

"Of course you were!" Sally's sarcasm continued.

"Cut it out you two," Rick reprimanded them. "Our real battle is coming in a few days' time. Perhaps I should take a nap."

"Help yourself," Jason said. "It's certainly better than being dead."

"Tell me about it," Rick said.

Rick tried to sleep through the road trip back, but it was easier said than done. He was too excited about the coming funeral service for him to doze off. As much as he tried, he kept waking up to the soft conversation between Jason and Sally. Perhaps trying to sleep at this time was futile. He decided to sit up and start talking with them again.

"How far are we?" he asked.

"It says here that we still have forty more minutes of driving," Sally said.

"Do we need to do something about our clothes for the service?" Jason asked.

"It would be great for me to wear a suit at my funeral, but I'm not dead," Rick said. "I think a living man in my outfit is way better than a dead man in a suit, what do you think?"

"Amen!" Jason said, incessantly grateful that his brother was still alive.

"Did you just say 'Amen'?" Rick asked.

"Yes sir, I did," Jason said.

"When did you have your 'come to Jesus' moment?" Rick asked.

"I really haven't made that decision, but I'm inching closer," Jason said.

"I sure hope you do so soon," Sally said. "I want a godly husband."

"What about you, Sally?" Jason asked. "Don't you think I want a godly wife?"

"Oh, I've already had my 'come to Jesus' moment," Sally said.

"Really?" Jason asked. "And when were you going to tell me about this?"

"I thought you already knew," Sally playfully said, punching him gently on his shoulder.

"Clearly, you two need to see a marriage counselor," Rick said.

"That's not the point," Sally pretended to be protesting. "Jason is supposed to know my likes and dislikes, my preferences and the things I disapprove of. He needs to know all these before we tie the knot."

"The door swings both ways," Jason said. "You need to know my likes and dislikes, my preferences, and the things I disapprove of. You need to know all these before we tie the knot."

She gave him a gentle punch on the shoulder "Use your own words." But as she punched him, the car swerved slightly, just in time to be seen by a state trooper waiting to stop speeding vehicles. Sally looked through her rearview mirror as she passed the trooper.

"Oh, no" she said. "That state trooper is slowly pulling onto the highway."

Rick was quite familiar with these drills. He advised everyone to stay calm. The trooper pulled Sally over. His lights were still on when he walked to Sally's window and asked for her license, insurance, and registration. She gently complied. He went back to his car and ran her plate. After a few minutes, which felt like an eternity to Sally, he came back to Sally, and handed the documents back to her.

"Do you know why I stopped you?" he asked.

"I'm afraid not," Sally said, "except for the slight swerve back there. It's the only reason I can think of."

"No, it's not that," he said. "Your left head lamp isn't working. Be sure to have it fixed."

"Oh! I didn't know that," Sally said. "I'll get it fixed right away."

"Have a good day, ma'am," the trooper said, "and be careful out there."

"Thank you!" Sally said.

It was now Jason's turn to make fun of Sally. "Who's the careless one now?"

"Oh, hush," Sally said. "It was just a busted head lamp. By the way, he didn't even seem to notice that you guys were in here."

"I'll have to admit that was close," Jason said. "You know I'm a wanted man."

"I agree. That was close," Rick said. "You know I'm a dead man. You don't carry dead people in the back seat of your car." They all laughed at Rick's humor. Not too long afterwards, they reached Sally's parents' house. It was 2 am Monday morning. Salley had called ahead to let them know they were on their way back. Perhaps they would have a few hours of sleep and rest before they could venture out for a week that was promising to be extremely eventful.

35

When Matthew and Sharon Roberts finished praying with Louella over the phone late Sunday night, they began to sense something going on in the spiritual realm. Having been a pastor at Rockville Community Church for several years, his experience exposed him to several supernatural encounters scientifically unexplainable but spiritually significant. What Louella seemed to be going through and the inner urge to pray for her during the vandalism of her flower shop left the impression on him that he was dealing with something deeply spiritual. Moreover, Sunday evening's prayer meeting in his office and Sunday night's teleconference with his wife and Louella impacted his personal prayer hour more profoundly than ever before. As he sat in his prayer closet, lifting Rockville Community Church before the Lord and reading Scripture to hear God's word, he sensed a deeper urge to continue praying for Rockville Community Church, for the funeral service to be held there on Wednesday, and for Louella. What a brave woman! She walked to the TV station and handed over the brown envelope with all its contents. That should ruffle some feathers.

"Are you coming to bed?" Sharon interrupted his thoughts as she opened the door to his prayer closet. "You've been in there for quite a while now. Is everything alright?"

"I'll be coming shortly," he replied. "I just need to think through the sermon I'll be delivering at the funeral service on Wednesday." Their two boys were already asleep. Sharon made sure to see them off to bed before focusing on her husband's concerns.

"Okay," Sharon said. "I'll wait for you."

"Thanks, honey," he said, as she shut the prayer closet door behind her.

"Lord," Matthew prayed, "what's the best approach for Wednesday's funeral sermon? I need your guidance. What Scripture should I use?" The events leading up to Sunday evening denied him the opportunity to work on the funeral sermon. The more he thought about it, the harder it got for him to put anything together. He remembered learning at seminary how, sometimes, pastors go through a period of sermon droughts before the inspiration to speak comes. Matthew wasn't sure he would overcome the drought he was facing.

"Lord," he kept praying, "please give me a word for your grieving people." He read the Scriptures, and prayed, and read, and prayed, and read, and nothing seemed to click.

Finally, as if to surrender everything to the Lord, he whispered a final prayer, saying, "Lord, it's all in your hands," closed his Bible, turned off his prayer closet lights, and stepped out of the room. Whenever he stepped out of his prayer room, he always felt an unexplainable sense of rejuvenation and strength. He always believed he could face any spiritual obstacle following the spiritual renewal in his prayer closet. Not tonight. He felt uncertain, hesitant, and somewhat subdued.

As he walked toward their bedroom, he found Sharon already in bed but still awake, reading her Bible. "Did you hear anything from the Lord?" she asked.

"So far, the Lord has kept it from me," he said. I feel kind of like Elisha when the Lord didn't reveal to him anything about the Shunammite woman's dead son in 2 Kings 4:18–37. For one reason or another, God is keeping the word from me. I think he will make it plain. He's never too early; he's never too late. He never comes at the eleventh hour. He comes right on time because . . ."

"The times are in his hands," Sharon completed the thought for him. She'd heard him speak numerous times, employing that exact line. Sometimes she even thought she could preach his sermons for him, but she wisely remained silent about that, especially when he seemed concerned that he had nothing to say about Wednesday's funeral service.

Matthew changed into his pajamas, brushed and flossed his teeth, cleaned his mouth with mouthwash, and was ready for bed. He held his wife's hands as they prayed together for the night, kissed her goodnight, and fell asleep. He looked at the clock. It said 12:30 am. It was Monday morning already! Not too long after drifting off to sleep, he became immediately aware of being in a hostile environment. Exactly where that was, he couldn't tell. It felt to him like he was in the middle of a brewing storm. The thunderclouds were gathering, and they seemed to be in layers. The lower layer up in the sky was dark gray, and above that layer was a lighter shade of gray but eerily similar to a funnel cloud. As he looked at the sky, he thought he saw a slithery, elastic lizard-like creature with the head of a cat coming toward him. He tried to run but couldn't. Something had immobilized him. He tried to move his hands, but, again, he couldn't. Whatever was going on around him had him pinned down on the ground and was beginning to choke him. He tried to say something, but he barely had the strength to speak. The creature, whatever it was, approached him with terrifying hostility. He knew at once that this was a spiritual attack from the dark world. *Resist the devil and he will flee away from you*, was the verse from James 4:7 that came to his mind. But he couldn't speak it. He decided to *think* it instead with all his being: *Spirit, go away in the name of Jesus*, he commanded in his mind. The creature turned around and screamed as if it had been hit by a pack of dynamite. Suddenly, Matthew regained his ability to move and speak.

This time he spoke out loud and said, "Spirit, go away in the name of Jesus!" His words startled Sharon.

"Honey," Sharon said, "what's going on? Are you alright?"

"I had a demonic attack," he said.

"You were struggling for about five seconds and then you said, 'Spirit go away.'"

"Yes," Matthew said. "I found myself in a hostile environment, as if I was in the midst of a storm, and this hideous lizard with the head of a cat came at me. I couldn't move or speak, so I rebuked the spirit in my mind and then rebuked it out loud as soon as I was able to speak. I apologize for startling you."

"That's not a problem at all, but what does this mean?" she asked.

"I think it means we're under some kind of evil attack," he said.

"Perhaps it would be a good thing to pray again," she offered. They prayed for each other and asked the Lord to send his angelic hosts to keep them out of harm's way. The prayer lasted for about ten minutes. When they felt relieved of their burden, they both said, "Amen."

"I wonder what the Lord is preparing for us in the coming days," Matthew said.

"You really think God is about to show up in some way?" Sharon asked.

"I'm sensing something," he said, "but I want to be cautious about it." Once again, he kissed her goodnight and went back to sleep. This time

Matthew slept like a baby. However, at about 6 am Monday morning, something startled him. He didn't know what it was. He looked at the clock. It said 6:01. He decided to get up and go to his prayer room. As he sat there, he prayed for the day's events and asked the Lord, once again, to preside over everything that was to happen at the church. As he prayed, John 11:25–26 came to mind: "I am the resurrection and the life. The one who believes in me will live, even though they die. And whoever lives and believes in me will never die. Do you believe this?" He wondered if that would supply the text for his message for Wednesday. He jotted a few words on a pad, developed an outline, and before he knew it, he was writing furiously until he heard his wife interrupting him with a shout.

"Honey!" She screamed, "Come quick! Action News was raided by the Rockville Police. It's about to run the story."

The pastor ran out of his office and glued his eyes onto the TV. He couldn't believe what he was watching. Did his dream last night have anything to do with this? He wondered as the news played itself right before his eyes. "I wonder if that's why I had that dream last night!"

"Honey, this is awful," Sharon said. "This is absolutely awful."

36

WHAT MATTHEW AND SHARON were watching on TV at 7:00 am on Monday began much earlier, around 2 am, with a certain kind of excitement, which was building up in the Action News station. Gloria Steele was preparing herself for a bombshell newscast that would, quite possibly, propel her to national fame. Today seemed to be her lucky day. She would likely cast herself as the lead investigator into a crime that brought down Rockville's most corrupt businessman as well as its most corrupt police officer. Everything had to be done in the right way. She had to inflect her voice at the right time, pause dramatically for effect, and use catchy phrases and expressions to keep viewers glued to their screens. This was her big day in many ways.

She made sure the cameras were accentuating her features correctly. She'd gone through prior facial makeup and hoped no wardrobe malfunction would rear its ugly head on such an important day. In addition, in two days her crew would have a field day at Rockville Community Church for the funeral of Detective Rick Mulley who was poisoned while trying to investigate the vandalism of a small business franchise downtown. The events couldn't have converged at a better time.

As Gloria's excitement grew bigger, another excitement was brewing outside the Action News premises. Following orders from police chief Drake Riley, a battalion of police officers in riot gear with guns drawn were preparing to raid the office. They'd been listening in on Jason Mulley's conversation with Louella Goodman, and they knew exactly what Louella had done. She'd surrendered the thumb drive they were looking for to Action News. They followed each other in single file, aiming their guns at the entrance to the news station.

Without warning, they busted the door open and yelled commands at the top of their voices.

"Everybody down!" one officer ordered.

"Lie down and don't move!" another one screamed.

"Everyone, hand over your cell phones!" still a third one said.

Some people yelled; others screamed. Some tried to escape through the front door, but they were repelled as if they hit a blank wall. Others shut themselves in the bathroom, pretending to use it. But they were roughly and quickly pulled out and ordered to get down on the floor.

"Let me see your hands!" one officer who appeared to be commanding the raid said. They lifted their hands in the air, as some were on their knees while others lay flat with their faces on the floor. The officers moved from one room to another, combing every area to make sure no one was hiding. They opened drawers and scattered important documents on the floor. They seemed to be looking for something specific—a thumb drive.

"Where is the thumb drive?" one officer asked. No one answered.

"I'll ask one more time," the officer yelled. "Where is the thumb drive?"

"What thumb drive?" a brave reporter tried to ask for clarification.

"The thumb drive that was brought here a few hours ago by some woman known as Louella Goodman," he said.

A few people seemed to know what he was talking about, so one person said, "It's in acquisitions."

"Okay," the policeman said. "Where is the acquisitions department?" No one answered. The silence was followed by the sound of guns cocking and, with them, terrified screams. "I said, where is the acquisitions department?"

One of the people lying on the ground nervously pointed down the hallway toward a library of videos, tapes, and books. Three officers went down the hallway, opened the door, and found one scared woman hiding under the table.

"You! Over there!" yelled the policeman. "I can see you. Come out from under that table and show me what I'm looking for." Nervously, Gloria Steele came out.

"I know you," said the policeman. "You're the morning show news anchor, Gloria Steele. Hand over the thumb drive that was brought here a few hours ago!"

"I don't know what you're talking about," said Gloria.

"Yes, you do. Louella Goodman gave it to you when she stopped here. Hand it over or I'll arrest you. You are illegally in possession of materials pertinent to an investigation we're conducting."

"As I said, I have no idea what you're talking about," Gloria responded.

"Maybe this will jog your memory," he said and showed her a video recording of her receiving a brown envelope from Louella Goodman. They had hacked into Action News's security cameras and obtained the video footage of the event.

"Now," the officer said slowly and deliberately, "Where is the thumb drive? I . . . want . . . it . . . now!" as he cocked his gun threatening to pull the trigger. "I'm not afraid to use this gun," he said. All the police officers conducting the raid were inside the building. It felt like a terrorist attack.

Gloria got on her feet and walked toward a drawer with the words "classified" labeled on it. She pulled out a brown envelope and handed everything to the three officers.

"Classified, my foot! Thank you very much," he said. "Now that wasn't too difficult, was it?" The officers walked away without waiting for Gloria to answer. As they walked back toward the reception area, they called off the raid.

The lead officer then announced to the employees, "All your cell phones are in this basket here. You can take them after we leave."

Turning to the others he said, "Mission accomplished. I have the documents. Back to the police station everybody. Nice job, all of you!" It was Chief Drake Riley. He had planned the raid and made sure the documents were all safely in his custody. What he forgot to bear in mind was the fact that Gloria Steele had already made copies of the documents and was still preparing to broadcast its contents. What made it even better was that the entire raid was recorded on Action News security video. The day turned out much better than she expected.

But the employees at Action News were visibly shaken. What has this country come to, they wondered, if freedom of the press could be violently taken away from them as was evident? This was not democracy. It wasn't what they signed up for as journalists. But if this was what it would take to regain control of their freedom, then so be it.

Meanwhile, as the policemen were heading back to the station, Chief Riley announced that they would be headed for the funeral in two days, all thirteen of them, to make some arrests. They were sure Jason Mulley would be there. They were sure Louella Goodman would be there. These two would be arrested for obstruction of justice. Therefore, he asked his officers to be prepared to do that immediately after the pastor's final word. Jason wouldn't be allowed to attend his brother's burial. Indeed, Jason himself knew he wouldn't be attending his brother's burial—something else, but not the burial!

37

When Monday morning arrived, there was no small commotion in Rockville, especially inside and outside Action News studios. Word about the raid had spread like wildfire. The employees of the studio, though quite rattled, managed to pick up the pieces of broken stuff, cleaned up the place, and braced themselves for war. Rockville Police Department had certainly won the battle, but they hadn't won the war. To be sure, the war had just begun. They were ready to go on air, and they had all the footage of the raid recorded neatly in their surveillance cameras. Moreover, a few of the camera crew with extensive experience in hostile situations and war zones sprang into action as the police raided their station. The crew was especially gifted in capturing crucial scenes without notice in times like these. What they put together all night seemed like a movie playing itself out in their very studios. If anything was going to propel Action News to fame, this was it!

At 6:30 am, Gloria Steele was ready. She had a change of clothes, put on fresh makeup and rehearsed the news of the morning with remarkable finesse. One wouldn't have imagined she was the victim. The different clips of the raid depicting the police brandishing their weapons, making their demands and insisting on the thumb drive were neatly edited and ready to run at a moment's notice. Gloria looked at her watch again. It was 6:37 am. Time was not going fast enough. She made several visits to the bathroom. Her anxiety was getting the better of her. She wasn't sure whether she needed a glass of water or a cup of coffee. Her tummy seemed too restless to allow her to ingest anything. She looked at her watch again. It was 6:39 am. *Why does time slow down when you need it to go fast?* she asked herself.

Jeffrey Brooks, the manager of the studio, stepped into the room. Obviously disturbed by the raid a few hours earlier, he gave Gloria a gentle side hug and an approving smile. He wasn't in the studio during the raid, but they had called him immediately after the police left the station, and he quickly drove to the studio.

"I'm sure you'll do well," he said with an assuring voice. "You always come out on top. Make us proud."

"Yes, sir," Gloria said. They had two big stories that morning: the raid and the scandal. Meanwhile, other stations nearby caught wind of the story. They too wanted to get a piece of the pie. A battery of journalists gathered outside Action News studios. The phone lines were jammed with calls from all over the country. Other stations wanted to know what was going on so they, too, could report it to their viewers.

The countdown to 7:00 am began. Gloria positioned herself at the news desk. First came the usual commercials from local car dealers enticing would-be customers to stop by their dealership for great deals and rates. Then came a cereal commercial followed by laundry soap commercials. And then a recorded teaser airing four minutes before showtime declared, "Coming up at 7 am, Rockville Police raided the Action Newsroom with guns drawn amid screams and panic. Also coming up at 7 am, a local business tycoon is implicated in a damning scandal that also involves Rockville Police Department. These stories and more coming up at 7 am. Don't go away."

Meanwhile, Matthew and Sharon stayed glued to their TV sets. Mason Kruger saw it as well. He stormed into Mr. Dupree's office, saying, "Would you believe it? Action News is doing a story on the police raid this morning. Where's the remote?" Indeed, most of Rockville was beginning to turn their TV sets to Action News.

"Are you serious?" Mr. Dupree asked. "I thought Chief Riley scared the daylights out of them. Give me that remote!" he ordered, snatching it from Mason's hand after he had already turned the TV on and was browsing to find Action News. The commercials were still on, so they waited impatiently for 7 am. Other employees at Dupree Enterprises' headquarters nervously stared at the TV, repeatedly shifting their gaze from Dupree and Mason to the TV and then back to Dupree and Mason. Nancy was also there, aghast at what they were about to see.

Jeff Brooks was standing behind the cameras. Ordinarily, he would watch everything either from his office or from the control room just to be sure everything was going well. Today, however, was special. He wanted to see it unfolding behind the cameras. He gave Gloria an assuring thumbs-up sign. More commercials followed. As 7 am approached, the videographer gave the countdown sign. Gloria positioned herself appropriately. The go-ahead signal was given as the Action News theme song played through the air. The anchor's camera turned on. Then it was Gloria's turn.

"Good Monday morning, citizens of Rockville. We have breaking news this Monday morning. Rockville Police Department conducted a raid right here at Action News earlier today amid screams, panic, and terror from our employees. The raid happened around 2 am and lasted about thirty minutes. Officer Drake Riley led the raid that sent all employees to the floor in panic. Some were on their knees while others lay flat on the ground in a posture of surrender following orders by the officers."

Gloria's image disappeared on the screen. It was replaced by prerecorded footage of the raid and commentary depicting Chief Riley cocking his gun. The recording captured at least one bullet bouncing off the wall and missing a female employee kneeling behind the reception desk. Other police officers could be seen brandishing their guns and pointing them at the employees who stayed down, terrified and traumatized. More footage, with additional commentaries followed with one employee after another being interviewed. They aired their views of what transpired early Monday morning. Terror, trauma, panic, and fear were words they used to describe the whole event.

Gloria came back on the screen and moved on to the next item on the news, namely, the suspected reason for the raid. "It is believed," Gloria's broadcast proceeded, "that Chief Drake Riley was looking for a thumb drive he and his officers thought contained sensitive documents under investigation by the Rockville Police Department." Airing the footage of her being held at gunpoint, Gloria announced, "Chief Riley held me at gunpoint and asked me to release the thumb drive, which I did. But what did the thumb drive contain that made thirteen police officers from Rockville Police Department descend on Action News?" she asked.

"We believe we have the answer," she said. "The thumb drive was given to us by Miss Louella Goodman, the business owner of Rockville's Finest Flowers. She had received this thumb drive from Jason Mulley, the brother of a now deceased police officer. That police officer was poisoned while investigating the vandalism that occurred at Rockville's Finest Flowers this past Tuesday. The police officer died while receiving treatment at Rockville Regional Hospital."

Gloria's commentary continued while featuring a video footage of the document and, immediately thereafter, a picture of James Dupree: "The contents of the thumb drive included text messages from the CEO of Dupree Enterprises, Mr. James Dupree, whose picture you see here, suggesting that he orchestrated the raid at Rockville's Finest Flowers by hiring two young men who then went ahead and vandalized the flower shop. The documents in that thumb drive indicate that Mr. Dupree, aided by his lawyer, Mason Kruger, paid the two young men five thousand dollars each to raid the flower shop. Mr. Dupree also paid Chief Drake Riley a large sum of hush money, fifteen thousand dollars to be exact, to keep the police from putting the crime under investigation. The documents in the thumb drive, as you can see here, also show that Rick Mulley, the detective who was investigating the crime at the flower shop, was poisoned because he was close to solving it, implicating Mr. Dupree, Mason Kruger, and Chief Drake Riley."

Gloria's image then came back onto the screen. "This," she said, "is the reason we believe the raid took place at Action News this morning. We'll be back after the commercial break."

That segment of the broadcast ended. The news coverage took a short commercial break to catch their breath as they prepared to move to the next item. Both Mr. Dupree and Mason Kruger turned deathly pale with fright. Mason ran to the bathroom to empty his bowels. Mr. Dupree was sweating bullets. For the first time in his life, he felt fear and terror gripping him. A major commotion ensued at Dupree Enterprises. The employees began to talk excitedly among themselves, trying to make sense of what they saw on TV. Action News was on air again after the commercial break. Gloria Steele was at her news desk. She announced that Detective Rick Mulley's funeral would be held at Rockville Community Church and that a large crowd was expected at the funeral specifically because Mulley was a well-loved and dedicated police officer. The newscast then switched to other items in the news that day.

But the broadcast left an indelible mark. The reporters outside were writing and typing furiously. They wanted to secure an interview with Gloria Steele. Others, not knowing whether they would catch Gloria, tried to interview any employee they could find. This stuff was going to sell like hot cakes, sending their ratings through the roof. Suddenly, what seemed a misfortune to Action News was beginning to look good for business.

Dupree Enterprises, however, was not doing too well. The employees went numb and froze with fear. What would happen to Dupree Enterprises? The news was disconcerting, and they had no idea what the next few days would look like.

Sam also got wind of the news and immediately called Louella.

"Louella," he said. "Did you see the news?"

"Yes, I did," she said. "The story about the raid took me by surprise. The story about the thumb drive didn't."

"Didn't you know about the raid?" Sam asked.

"No, I didn't, but I am not surprised it happened. Those guys followed me when I went down to the news station to hand them the thumb drive."

"You took the thumb drive to the station?" Sam asked.

"Yes, I did," she replied.

"You didn't tell me you had this information with you," he said.

"For some reason I thought you knew I had the information," she said. "But I knew I had to speak up. Something had to be done."

Sam was in a dilemma. The pieces of the puzzle that Mason talked about were now in place. His uncle was behind the raid. He couldn't deny that. The woman he was really beginning to like, and possibly court, blew the whistle on his uncle. Whose side should he take? If he took his uncle's side, he'd be siding with a criminal. If he took Louella's side, he'd be turning his back on his family. He didn't know how to handle the situation, but then he thought more deeply about it. If his uncle was found guilty, which seemed very likely, possibly even a foregone conclusion, then his uncle would go to prison for a long time. Creating an environment where a police officer was murdered is no small crime. You don't kill a police officer. Period. That's simply a no-go zone. As difficult as it may seem, he chose the side of justice.

"Louella," Sam said, "I'm on your side. For a long time, I've watched my uncle get away with murder. He wasn't going to stop until something stopped him. It seems to me this is it for him. He'll more than likely go behind bars. I don't want to be a part of that. I want to be an upright citizen. Would you help me become one?"

"Yes, of course," Louella said. "I'll be of help to you in any way I can. But if you really want me to help you, you must begin by coming to church with me every Sunday. By the way, will you be coming to the funeral on Wednesday at 10 am? It's the only way we can honor Detective Mulley."

"I would love to," he said. "See you then." They ended the conversation, and Louella sat pensively in her living room, amazed at the quick turn of events. This was going to be another interesting day just like the day before. Action News ran that story repeatedly throughout the day. Other news channels picked up from where Action News left off. It was beginning to look really bad for Drake Riley. Major news agencies descended on the Rockville Police Department. They proceeded with caution, though, knowing what some of the officers there were capable of. Brave reporters, however, accosted different police officers returning to the station from field assignments. But those officers were under strict instructions not to engage the reporters in any conversations. Rockville Police Department appointed a spokesperson for the entire operation. For the most part, though, he remained tight-lipped when answering specific questions about the raid because, as he said, "the matter was still under investigation."

38

THROUGHOUT THE DAY ON Monday, the FBI in Lockridge prepared to make several major arrests in Rockville. They had gathered enough material and assigned various federal agents the task of arresting those involved in the vandalism of Rockville's Finest Flowers shop, owned by Louella Goodman. Larry and Hank bragged about raiding Louella's flower shop. Federal agents had tracked them down. They knew where Larry and Hank lived. Detective Rick Mulley had stopped by their home several days prior, but no arrests had been made. A warrant for their arrest had now been issued.

On Tuesday morning, at 8 am, the agents went up the steps leading to Larry and Hank's door. As they approached it, they heard a commotion inside the house. Two individuals inside the home seemed to be having an altercation. They seemed to be arguing about a raid they did a few days ago.

"We can't keep doing Mr. Dupree's dirty work for him," one protested, sounding like he was pushing a wooden piece of furniture violently toward his mate. It seemed to hit the hard wooden door with a sickening crash.

"Oh no, you don't, Larry," his mate said. "How dare you hurl that chair at me. You're not getting away that easily. We have to finish off the work."

"I'm not your partner, Hank," Larry said. "I'll not be party to these operations anymore. Last Thursday's break-in was the last. If Mr. Dupree wants to keep attacking people, let him do it himself."

"It's too late for you to back off, Larry," Hank said. "If you're in, you're in. Back out of this at your own risk."

"How dare you!" Larry said. "I'm gonna give you a couple of lumps," he said as sounds of violently moving furniture came through the open window. They were wrestling each other. Amid loud sounds of *ouch* and *oof* and *eek* and *akh*, they seemed to be punching, kicking, smacking, and elbowing each other. "You'll pay for this!" Larry kept saying.

"I aint payin' you nuthin!'" Hank responded, and the punching seemed to go on. A shot rang out. Whoever it was meant to hit, it missed and went through the glass window, narrowly missing the federal agents outside.

The agents looked at each other and, as if on cue, drew their guns, approaching the door carefully. "Federal agents!" they announced themselves. One of the agents then kicked the door open and marched inside just in time to see two men running for their lives through the back door, shooting back at them and then jumping over the backyard, wire-meshed fence and into the backyard of their neighbor's property. The neighbor's dog barked excitedly from its kernel. They kept running beside the house, each on either side, from the back to the front, toward the front lawn and onto the street.

"Stop!" the agents ordered. "Stop running. You're under arrest." But the two young men kept running. They weren't about to give up that easily. Since they were youthful enough, they believed they could outrun the agents, but the agents had been trained for just these kinds of scenarios and knew exactly what to do. Without wasting much time, the federal agents started off in hot pursuit. The individuals didn't get very far. As Larry was trying to outrun both officers, they caught up with him and knocked him down from behind.

"Oof," was the sound that came out of Larry's mouth as he went tumbling on the lush lawn of the property across the street. The other man kept running, but the second agent caught up with him and knocked him down with the same technique. As each was cuffed, the agents asked them for their names. The first one was named Larry, and the second Hank. The agents read them their rights, and frog-marched them to the FBI van. The two were safely in custody and would be facing the full force of the law.

Meanwhile, at Dupree Enterprises, panic filled the air. James Dupree was anything but calm. He couldn't stomach the thought of seeing his name implicated in the vandalizing of the flower shop. He was hysterical that the news station cast him in such a bad light. Mason Kruger was literally sick. Mr. Dupree needed to remain constantly aware of the updates, what the news was saying, and whether the Rockville Police Department would turn its back on him. He vowed to be at the funeral service on Wednesday at Rockville Community Church to witness the possible arrests of everyone undermining his efforts to take over Rockville.

Just then he heard a knock at his door. "Are we expecting anyone?" he asked Mason who was in the adjacent office.

"No, sir," said Mason. "I'll answer it." When he opened the door, he saw several FBI agents standing outside, possibly four or five of them. He wasn't very sure from his vantage point exactly how many they were. Behind them, however, was a battery of journalists covering the potential arrest as it unfolded.

"Hello," said one of the agents, "Are Misters James Dupree and Mason Kruger in?"

"Who wants to know?" Mason asked as the cameras flashed incessantly, blinding his vision.

All the agents whipped out their badges and said, "We're federal agents." More cameras flashed and microphones descended like tentacles toward Mason.

"Is everything alright, Mason?" asked Mr. Dupree who had stepped out of his office and walked through the reception area to see what was going on. On hearing Mr. Dupree's voice, the journalists inched closer, holding their microphones as close to the door as they could possibly get.

"Are you Mr. Dupree, sir?" asked one of the agents.

"Yes, I am," Mr. Dupree said.

"And who is Mason Kruger? asked another federal agent.

"I am," Mason answered.

"Mr. Dupree, we are placing you under arrest for attempted murder of a police officer, for aiding and abetting the breaking and entering of Rockville's Finest Flower shop, and for fraudulent mutilation of a title owned by Louella Goodman." As they cuffed him, one federal agent read him his rights. The journalists moved forward, some almost losing their footing from being pushed by other journalists dying to cover the entire story as it unfolded. The cameras continued to click and flash.

Mr. Dupree protested furiously, screaming obscenities at them. "Wait until you hear from my lawyer, sirs," he said. "You have no evidence and no right to arrest me."

"Wait until you hear what we have on you," the agents said. "We'll make sure you remain behind bars for years."

"I'll call Chief Riley to arrest you all," Mr. Dupree went on.

"Oh, he's in trouble, too," said another agent. "Wait until you hear what we've got on him."

They bundled Mr. Dupree into the back of their van, securely in their custody, and drove off.

"Mr. Dupree, did you orchestrate the vandalism at Rockville's Finest Flowers?" one journalist asked.

"Mr. Dupree, did you pay Chief Riley the hush money to keep him quiet?" another one asked.

"Mr. Dupree, what will become of your business following this bombshell?" still another journalist fired her question.

Mr. Dupree was too numb to hear and too vexed to answer. A crowd had camped outside Dupree Enterprises all day on Monday more out of curiosity than anything else. They had seen the 7 am news item that morning, and they wondered how the people at Dupree Enterprises were handling the whole situation. As Mr. Dupree was being led away, the cameras were rolling—cell phone cameras, social media live feeds, and out of state news stations. Some of the observers were excited that a notorious criminal had at last been arrested. Others were sad that a major revenue earner for Rockville, Dupree Enterprises, could actually shut down, and still others were unsure of what to make of it. They adopted a wait and see approach. Perhaps that was more prudent for them, but they were erring on the side of caution.

39

All Pastor Matthew could think of all day on Tuesday was the Action News 7 am broadcast from the previous morning. Every time he thought about it, he reacted to it as if he was seeing it for the very first time. "What in the world was that?" he asked for the umpteenth time.

Sharon responded, "I know. This is absolutely bizarre."

"Tell me about it," Matthew said. "The Lord was sending us a warning all along. The spiritual attack from early Sunday morning, the prayer for Jason's safety, the prayer for Louella—all these seemed to point toward something. Could this be it?"

"I think something else is brewing," said Sharon, who seemed especially perceptive in such matters. "Don't be surprised if something dramatic happens at the funeral service tomorrow."

"Oh! The funeral service!" Matthew said. "I'd forgotten about that!"

"You'd better not," Sharon said. "Even the news item ran a story on it."

"I was so transfixed by the raid that it almost escaped my mind," Matthew said as he ran back to his prayer closet. He needed to finish the sermon he was putting together. He sat down and worked on the sermon from John 11:25–26. As he read the text, he felt the need to bring encouragement to the community. He decided to base his entire sermon on the text from John 11:17–24. He would make six short points: Jesus feels your pain because (1) he comes, (2) he comforts, (3) he calls, (4) he cares, (5) he cries, and (6) he cures. He just needed to give each point a short explanation, a short illustration, and a short application. If he gave each point three minutes, with a three-minute introduction and a three minute conclusion, he would have a 24-minute sermon. That would be sufficient to keep everyone's attention focused on what he needed to say. What was left for him to do was to memorize the text and the entire sermon. It was around 8 am. He had two hours to do so before heading out to church for a series of meetings with the staff. He wasn't sure he would accomplish that feat, but he tried.

After one hour of trying to memorize the text, Sharon knocked at his office door.

"Honey," she said, "don't you think we should head out to church now?"

Matthew was somewhat startled. He wasn't expecting a knock at his door, not because he didn't want to be reminded but merely because he was so engrossed in the process of memorizing the text that he lost track of time.

"Sure," he said. "I'll get my collar and jacket right away."

Before too long, they were pulling away from the driveway to head to church. Rockville Community Church was only about seven minutes away, so they thought they would be arriving in good time. As they approached the sanctuary, they imagined how packed the parking lot would be Wednesday. Many people would be coming for the service, and the police officers would be directing traffic. Sharon and Matthew weren't sure whether the officers would be there to make further arrests or whether they would really be there to help with the funeral service. The question, perhaps, didn't matter since the Rockville Police Department had scheduled the service.

Pastor Matthew had spent most of the day on Monday putting together the order of service, sending it to Chief Riley who approved it and sent it back to him. It was going to be a very simple service. They would have the words of welcome, an opening hymn, Scripture reading, another hymn, and then words of encouragement from family, from friends, and from the chief of police himself. After another hymn, Pastor Matthew would bring the message and close the service.

As he parked his car at the pastor's spot, he noticed, to his slight shock, a considerably high number of journalists positioning their cameras at strategic points around the church premises. Some were standing in front of the cameras and speaking into a microphone, more than likely recording the proceedings as they unfolded for a live feed or a later broadcast. Matthew and Sharon were sure they didn't want anything to do with the journalists at this point when so much was at stake. Both of them weren't sure how the day would pan out. Would it be an absolute disaster following the raid at Action News, or would it have something redemptive to it? These questions swirled around their minds, and each one knew what the other was thinking. They'd been married for eight years, and in those eight years of marriage, they had grown in their love and appreciation for each other beyond the typical romance found among young couples. Admittedly, though, Sharon knew her husband more than her husband knew her. They did have their challenges as a couple, of the sort anyone would find in any marriage—fights, irritations, children, finances. But through those challenges, they learned to grow together as God's servants.

They tried to ignore the reporters. They were extremely grateful the reporters didn't know them. Pastor Matthew quickly removed his clerical collar to avoid getting noticed. They then pretended not to be people of much significance in the church and walked right past the journalists who seemed to have camped there all night into Tuesday morning. Matthew and Sharon desperately hoped they would avoid the reporters, and they did. When they walked into the building, they met with the staff members and made the plans for conducting the funeral the following day. Mr. Smith would lead the service and congregational singing while Jeremy Jones would read Scripture. Everything seemed to be in place for Wednesday. After having a few more meetings with congregation members who came to see him for counseling, Pastor Matthew and Sharon headed back home. It had been a surprisingly calm day—very likely, the calm before the storm.

40

WEDNESDAY MORNING ARRIVED SOONER than either Pastor Matthew or Sharon would have liked. Neither was looking forward to that day. Sharon fixed breakfast for her husband only to remember that ordinarily he liked to eat after a speaking event rather than before for two reasons: First, it was his way of fasting before a major spiritual task because he wanted to have the correct spiritual wavelength between him and God, and second, he didn't want to wrestle with an upset stomach arising from the anxiety of preaching. Sharon put everything in the fridge in the hope that her husband would eat it later. They quickly pulled out from the driveway after cleaning their teeth and headed to the church. Once again, they arrived sooner than either of them wanted. Pastor Matthew's seminary professor had reminded him such days would come at least once in his ministry.

The parking lot, as expected, was full, mostly of members of the congregation who knew Rick Mulley. However, a huge portion of the attendees were out-of-town guests, mostly blood relatives of Rick. A considerable number of officers from the Rockville Police Department were on the scene, some, about thirteen of them, in their official uniforms. One would have expected a larger number to be in uniform as a way of honoring their fallen colleague. However, there was a much larger number from that department in plainclothes. Chief Riley was there. He seemed to have parked his car in a conspicuous place for reasons best known to him. The journalists Pastor Matthew saw the previous day were still there. They'd been running stories about the upcoming funeral since Monday night into Tuesday morning and proceeded to do the same thing all day on Tuesday. Whatever would transpire today was something they didn't want to miss.

As both Sharon and Matthew stepped out of the car, Pastor Matthew's phone rang. Jason was calling, much to Pastor Matthew's horror.

"Jason!" Pastor Matthew answered, not sure how Chief Riley would take it if he knew about the call. "Where are you?"

"Oh, I'm on my way to church," Jason said.

Pastor Matthew sounded surprised, "You are? Aren't you afraid of being arrested?"

"No, I'm not," he said, "and wait until I show you what I have."

"Oh, Jason," Matthew moaned. "You're not coming to cause trouble, are you?"

"No, Pastor," Jason said. "I'm not coming over to cause trouble at all. I'm coming to stop trouble!"

"Now, Jason," Matthew protested, "I hate scenes. I fall apart at the sight of my own blood. Please behave yourself when you get here. I know it's your brother's funeral, but please do nothing that will cause trouble in this church."

"I assure you, pastor," Jason responded, "I won't even lift a finger when you see me. Everything will speak for itself, I promise you."

"You'd better be right," Matthew said.

"I know I'm right," Jason said with a little chuckle at the end of the sentence and hung up.

"Is everything alright?" Sharon asked.

"Jason is coming to the funeral," Matthew said.

"Oh, honey," Sharon said. "Under the circumstances, he shouldn't really be here. He'll get arrested. But it is his brother's funeral. He does have the right to be here."

"That's certainly the dilemma I'm facing," Matthew said. "I can't tell him not to come. All I can tell him is to do nothing that will cause mayhem here. We already have journalists eager to absorb everything that will be unfolding. I don't want us to give them fodder for propaganda."

As he said that, they walked into the building through the back door of the sanctuary so they could slip into Matthew's study unnoticed. They were wrong. Chief Riley was at the door of the study waiting for the pastor to show up.

"Hi, Rev.," he said. "Are you ready for the service?"

"Yes, sir," said the pastor. He wasn't sure he wanted to ask him about the Monday early morning raid. What he was sure about was the fact that he was standing next to a very corrupt man if what the news said that Monday morning was anything to go by. "I just need to get myself situated, and I'll be ready for the service."

"Suit yourself, sir," Chief Riley said. "We'll be out in the sanctuary if you need us."

"I'll be sure to sing out when I need your input on anything," Matthew said.

As they stepped into the office, Sharon said, "I'm not really comfortable near that guy anymore. Did you see how he conducted himself on Sunday at the church service?"

"Yes," said Matthew. "It was awful how they handled Louella."

The sanctuary was full. There was very little room for additional guests into the sanctuary. A TV screen was set for the overflow crowd in the fellowship hall. Even there, space was filling up very quickly. Rick Mulley's casket was lying at the very front of the church just before the stage area. It was a closed casket, as per the family's request. There would be no viewing. That was the set of instructions given to the funeral home. The funeral director did his due diligence in ensuring the casket was securely closed. No one was allowed to look inside.

More people kept coming into the sanctuary, including journalists who were quite content to sit on the carpet floor. Sam Palmer was there. He had come in an hour earlier for fear of not finding a good seat. He sat quietly off to one side and watched the proceedings from afar. Behind him was Louella Goodman. She too came in early, wanting to make sure she got a choice seat. Sally had come in with her parents. They were very interested in seeing how things would unfold, since they saw Rick, whom they thought was dead but were shocked beyond belief to see him walk right into their living room. He had taken a quick shower and changed clothes, which he borrowed from Sally's dad. They were of roughly the same size, and her dad's outfit did fit him perfectly. Sally's dad was tapping three of his fingers on the pews nervously as her mom leaned on his shoulder observing the stage, the casket, the lights, the movement of the organist from the piano to the organ and back to the piano to consult with the pianist. The prelude began with somber music as a slide show of Rick's pictures featured on the overhead screen. It was, in every way, a funeral service except the body wasn't there and only a few people knew of its whereabouts.

Law enforcement officers sat off to one side. Led by Chief Riley, one could see them talking solemnly to each other, nodding here, gesturing there, clasping their hands together, sometimes shaking their heads. Slipping in unnoticed, however, were federal agents from Lockridge—a horde of them. They positioned themselves directly behind and beside the law enforcement officers, especially the ones who conducted the raid. For some reason, the news station raiding officers stuck together. They made it very easy for the federal agents to spot them.

As 10 am approached, Pastor Matthew and his wife, Sharon, stepped out of the office. His deacon, Mr. Smith, and Julie, Mr. Smith's wife, were following closely behind. They took their places on stage as the prelude was playing. Pastor Matthew looked across at the organist. He was thankful for her. She was always on top of things. He looked across to the left and saw the pianist also following along with his accompaniment. He wished his services would be this full every Sunday. The clock struck 10, and the prelude trailed off to silence as Pastor Matthew took his position at the pulpit.

The mood was solemn. A police officer had fallen. He did his best to remain upbeat while capturing the mood simultaneously. He followed the order of service to the letter. It began with words of welcome followed by a word of prayer. As he looked at the order of service after prayer, he invited Mr. Smith to lead in the congregational singing. Jeremy Jones, who was seated with the congregation, read the Scripture. He read with authority as if he had written those words himself.

The second hymn followed, and Mr. Smith was back at the podium again, leading the singing. The service ran smoothly. When it was time for family to speak, Rick's brother, Jason, was nowhere to be seen. However, Rick's distant relatives who had come from out of town, expressed their profound shock, grief, and sorrow. Some of them wished they could have one final glance of Rick before his interment, but they understood Rick's wishes and wanted to honor them,

The time came for members of the Rockville Police Department to express their words of encouragement. Those who had worked with him as partners got to stand up first. They had nothing but praise for Rick. Some of their words were humorous; some were profound. Others were filled with grief and pain.

Chief Riley's time to speak came and he stood up to say something. His words were eloquent, precise and well calculated. He had his nuances in the right places; his gestures were well choreographed. One wouldn't have imagined that this same gentleman was the one behind the raid at Action News. He offered to assist Rick's family members, wherever they were, in any way they needed assistance. If anyone doubted Riley's showmanship, his presentation put everything to rest at that very hour. As soon as he was done, some members of the Rockville Police Department gave him a standing ovation, and he sat down.

One more hymn followed to prepare the congregation for the pastor's words. Pastor Matthew acknowledged the impact Rick had in the community, and the low profile he played as a member of Rockville Community Church. He knew Rick was devout in his faith, but he was also firm in his principles. He then went to his words of encouragement and gave the most passionate sermon he had ever given at any funeral service anywhere. His presentation was deeply moving. The congregation hung on his every word. His last point was even more emphatic: Jesus feels your pain because he cures us. He anchored that point on Jesus' command to Lazarus as he lay in the grave saying, "Lazarus, come out."

"Scripture says," continued Pastor Matthew, "'The dead man came out with his hands and feet wrapped with strips of linen.'" Pastor Matthew kept going: "Raising a dead man from the grave isn't too difficult for God to do. He can do it. Someday, you and I will be raised from the dead, and then all of us will experience what Lazarus experienced. The only difference is this: Lazarus died again, even after he was raised from the dead. But when we all rise again at the last day, we will never die again." The pastor concluded his sermon.

Before he sat down, he saw someone walk into the sanctuary from the back and slowly approach the front. Pastor Matthew's jaw dropped. *It can't be*, he thought to himself. *That man looks like Rick*! As the man approached the casket, everyone looked back to see what the pastor was looking at with his mouth open wide. Rick was walking to the front. Members of the police force began to murmur, which got increasingly louder, evolving into shouts and screams.

"Quiet!" Pastor Matthew said. "Quiet, please!" But even he didn't know what else to say. Rick walked all the way to the stage. Chief Riley's limbs were trembling. His hands were shaking. He tried to step outside, but he was intercepted by federal agents. As some of his officers began to approach the stage, the federal agents who had planted themselves in strategic places in the congregation blocked them, flashing their badges and gently telling them, "Please remain seated until we tell you to move. We're the FBI."

"Thank you all for attending my funeral," Rick said from the pulpit. Pastor Matthew was visibly shocked. He had no idea his last point would have direct relevance to what was playing itself out. The cameras were rolling. The police officers were trying to reach Rick for no apparent reason.

Rick went on speaking, "As you probably heard, I was poisoned and left for dead. I'm supposed to be inside that casket. Clearly, I am not. Someone wanted me dead. But the grace of God kept me from dying. I'm here because God gave me one more chance to live. When God gives you the chance to live and do something worthwhile for him, don't blow it. The pastor reminded us that Jesus feels our pain because he cures us. I was cured by Jesus, and I'm ready to serve him all the days of my life. When someone wants you dead, God will keep you deathless if it's not your time to go!"

Even though Rick Mulley didn't technically die, Pastor Matthew was so delighted that he came back from the dead. Matthew and Sharon walked up to him and gave him a tight bear hug. Smith and Jeremy Jones did the same. People began to run toward the stage to catch a glimpse of Rick. They hadn't seen anything like that before. The congregation began to sing, "When We All Get to Heaven," as if it was a revival service. The crowd began to swell at the front of the sanctuary as people flocked to the stage, hysterically and triumphantly. It was massive confusion, a sweet one!

Meanwhile, the federal agents began leading thirteen police officers out of the building, including Chief Riley. Once outside, the agents arrested them for gross misconduct, corruption, and use of highly excessive force. Chief Riley and his cohorts were led away. His assistant became the interim police chief as they sorted out the mess in the police department. Thankfully, only a small portion of the members of the Rockville Police Department were engaged in Mr. Dupree's shady deals. Since the remaining members of the police force were their subordinates, they couldn't do much, as Detective Rick Mulley later testified.

Back in the sanctuary, a revival was brewing. People were singing and clapping and jumping and praising God. Rick Mulley was among them. As tears flowed freely from his eyes, he shook hands and hugged those he knew. Louella Goodman happened to be there. She ran to the front and gave him a tight hug.

"I'm so sorry I couldn't solve your case for you," Rick said. "But I understand you took matters into your own hands and did some really fine investigative work there." Rick was just being polite.

"Oh, but you did solve the case, Rick," Louella said. "I'm so glad to see you. Welcome back from the dead!"

"Technically, I didn't die," he said. "I was poisoned, and I'm still weak from the poisoning. But I'm doing well, I promise you."

Jason walked toward the pastor and said, "Well, Pastor, did I behave myself?"

"You sure did, Jason," the pastor said. "You're a man of your word."

They talked as more people began to run into the sanctuary. The overflow crowd in the fellowship hall could no longer stay in there. They wanted to be at the center of the action. Why watch from a distance when everyone else was standing inside the sanctuary? Indeed, no one was sitting. This was standing room only, literally. As the crowd from the fellowship hall ran into the building, they joined in singing, "When We All Get to Heaven." The organist and the pianist kept playing the song. When they sang through the verses, the congregation started singing all over again. After they had done it three times, someone went to the pianist and asked if he needed a break.

"Absolutely," he said, "I want to sing not play." He slipped out of the piano as the substitute took over. No one knew him. The pastor had never seen him before. Jason looked at him and gasped. This was the same person who handed the phone to him during the accident! The gentleman appeared from nowhere and is now playing the piano like a pro! He looked at Jason and gave him a wink and kept playing. Someone else walked toward the organist and asked if she needed help.

"Yes, sir," she said. "I want to sing with everyone else." She slipped off her bench as the substitute took over. No one had seen the organist before. Both of them played as the congregation kept singing. More people came into the sanctuary more out of curiosity than anything else. As soon as they walked in, however, they seemed to walk into something—a deeply profound and unexplainable presence.

Jason was on his knees, his hands raised, with tears flowing down his face—tears of joy as he said, "Jesus, I love you! I love you! I believe! I believe." Sally and her parents ran by his side and joined him with hands raised in praise and thanksgiving.

People began flocking to the altar. Hands were raised. Some lay flat with their faces on the ground on the carpet floor. Others were on their knees. Many were on their feet, singing and jumping and praising God. Pastor Matthew began praying for those at the altar. He noticed someone else praying for a few others at the altar, and he just let them pray. A few more came and stood with those kneeling by the altar rails. The cries, the prayers, and the singing were all intense. God was moving in their midst. Who would have thought that a policeman's near death could orchestrate such an outpouring?

Rick's family from out of town were standing around him. They hadn't seen anything like this before. They came to a funeral, but they got a revival. They were beyond delighted to see their loved one again. That explained to them why the casket was closed.

"It can stay closed," they said. "We have our Rick." They hugged him, and cried, and hugged, and cried, and hugged again. They just couldn't have enough of him.

"This is what will happen when we get to heaven," they observed. The singing hadn't stopped. Jason looked up from the rails to see if the pianist was still playing. Yes, he was, hammering away at those keys. He looked across at the substitute organist. He was still playing, enjoying every minute of it. What a great conclusion to something that had played itself out so dangerously for him.

The journalists looked confused. Their cameras kept rolling, but most had no idea what was happening. They kept trying to secure interviews, asking, "What does this mean?" No one could really capture it in words intelligible to the journalists.

"It's a revival," one said.

"It's a move of the Holy Spirit," another interjected.

"We're just having a great time with the Lord," still others insisted.

"Have you ever seen anything like this before?" some journalists asked.

"Of course!" said one.

"Not in my lifetime?" said another.

"It's there in the Bible," still another insisted. "Read it and you'll see."

As they struggled to cover the events, they realized they were witnessing something unique, and they let it take its own identity. One of them walked over to Rick Mulley. She found it rather intriguing that Rick had walked into his own funeral and was eager to interview him.

"Sir," she said, "is it true that you were poisoned and left for dead?"

"Yes, ma'am," Rick said. "It's actually a miracle that I'm still alive."

"What if someone says all this was a ploy to get some attention? What would you say to that person?" she asked.

Rick responded. "It would be a very risky ploy to ingest potassium cyanide just to get some attention. You can't make this stuff up. And you know what, you will always have the skeptics doubting everything they see, read, or hear about. I'm not that kind of person."

"I'm sure this is a very meaningful day for you sir," she said, "and thank you very much for being willing to talk to me." She then walked away, and Rick continued visiting with his family.

The reporters tried to locate Matthew, the senior pastor of Rockville Community Church. They couldn't reach him. He was busy laying hands on those at the altar and praying for them. Just when they thought he was done, he quickly moved to the next person. Another person, who appeared to be a minister, was also doing his spiritual rounds, much like doctors did their medical rounds, moving from one person to another.

Suddenly, Jason gave a loud gasp. He was looking at his arm. The cut he got from the twisted metal at the accident scene was gone! "This can't be!" he said. "Sally cleaned up the wound when we got home from Lockridge. It was raw with blood on it!"

Sally rushed toward him to look. "Wow! How did that happen? The wound is gone!" Jason wondered if the substitute pianist had anything to do with it. He, too, was gone. He had already switched places with the church pianist and slipped out unnoticed. He ran over to the pianist and asked, "Where did your substitute pianist go?"

"He excused himself and stepped out of the sanctuary," the pianist said. Jason ran out of the sanctuary and headed to the restrooms to see if he could find the gentleman. The men's restroom was empty. He ran back into the sanctuary to see if he was back in there.

"Has anyone seen the substitute pianist?" he asked. No one could tell him where the man went.

Jason remembered his words: "If you need me, just call me." *But how can I call him if I don't know his name?* He wondered. *I don't even have his contact information.* As he kept on looking for the pianist, more and more people were flocking to the altar. Word had spread throughout Rockville that something strange was going on at Rockville Community Church. People were coming in to see the phenomenon.

Sam Palmer found himself kneeling at the altar. What he was experiencing moved him to sense the reality of a higher power in the room. Perhaps this higher power is what Pastor Matthew was talking about. Louella saw him kneeling by the rails and walked over to him. Then she knelt beside him. Sam didn't know what to do next. He just bowed his head, waiting for something to happen. Then he felt a hand on his left shoulder. Sam didn't look up. He was just happy that someone was praying for him.

The voice that came behind him sounded slightly different than Pastor Matthew's voice, but it spoke with authority: "I pray for Sam, Father, and ask you to touch every aspect of his life, including his work as a wedding planner and his hobby as a fitness trainer. I pray that he would surrender all these to you." Then just as suddenly, the hand seemed to move to the next person. Another hand touched his right shoulder. It was Louella. She did say something, except Sam didn't really hear it. But when she was done, they all said, "Amen," and went and sat down.

"That was awfully nice of Pastor Matthew to pray for me like that," Sam whispered to Louella.

"You must be mistaken," Louella said. "Pastor Matthew was on the far-left side of the sanctuary praying for other people as I prayed for you."

"No, no!" he said. "You don't understand. Pastor Matthew prayed for me. His hand was on my left shoulder as I bowed my head in prayer."

"Sam," Louella was emphatic. "Pastor Matthew was nowhere near you when we were at the altar. My eyes were open most of the time as I looked around to see who could come to pray with us. Pastor Matthew and the other minister are still praying for the people to the far left of the sanctuary, and they are working their way to the right. Pastor Matthew didn't pray for you at all."

"Then who was that praying for me?" he asked. "I distinctly heard a voice and felt a hand on my shoulder! I'm telling you, someone prayed for me. He prayed for my work as a wedding planner and for my fitness training gigs. I assumed you told Pastor Matthew about me. No one else in this room has this information about me."

Louella was stunned. "Sam!" she said. "It looks like we just had a visitation from the Lord himself!"

Sam was still new to this experience. What Louella said sounded like nonsense, but then he couldn't discount the experience he had.

"What do I need to do?" Sam asked.

"I think," Louella said, "you need to surrender every part of your life to the Lord, for starters."

"What does that mean?" he asked.

"It means being born again, inviting Jesus Christ into your heart, and believing that he died for you," Louella said.

"And how, exactly, am I supposed to do that?" he asked. Louella then explained to him the way of the cross and the exact words he needs to say. Simply say, "Lord Jesus, I realize that I am a sinner. I ask you to forgive me for my sins. I invite you into my heart as Lord and Savior." When you pray such a simple prayer, you begin a journey you'll never forget."

Sam was ready. "Can you help me say this prayer?"

"I'd be honored to," Louella said. She asked Sam to repeat the prayer after her. He repeated it and invited Jesus Christ into his heart. Louella broke down and cried tears of joy. She never expected she would ever play the significant role of leading Sam to faith in Jesus Christ.

Sam and Jason weren't the only ones surrendering their lives to Christ. Countless others were doing so at the altar. Some were surprised by the disappearance of pain in their bodies, including some members of the congregation who came in wheelchairs and using walkers the previous Sunday. Louella felt some warmth on her elbow. When she looked at it, the bruise from the fall she took outside her shop was completely gone.

"Holy Christ!" She gasped. "The wound on my elbow is gone," she yelled.

Others were overwhelmed by the presence of the Lord in the room. The crowd was getting too much for Pastor Matthew to handle. Some ministers from neighboring churches heard about the happenings. They came in and sat at the back to watch the proceedings. When they saw Pastor Matthew and the other minister getting overwhelmed, they asked if they could help.

"By all means," Pastor Matthew said. "We need all the help we could get." Sharon was beginning to get concerned about her husband. It was 3 pm, two hours after the service ended, and the crowd wasn't letting up. The ministers took over from Pastor Matthew and continued praying for those at the altar. Typically, Wednesdays weren't church days, but God was moving among his people. The sanctuary was still full. The casket was still lying there. The funeral director consulted with Rick and instructed him to return for the casket the following day.

As time went on, more journalists arrived. They heard about a dead man who was now walking, and they wanted to get a video recording of the person. In their eagerness, they found themselves walking into a revival. Parking was difficult to find. They had to park their vans a few hundred yards away and walk to the sanctuary. As with the earlier journalists, when they arrived, they didn't know what to do with what they witnessed unfolding before their eyes. People were praying. Some were singing. Several ministers were kneeling with those at the altar, laying hands on some, holding hands with others, raising hands in prayer, and everything in between.

The event continued into the early evening. Several people coming from work stopped by the church to witness for themselves what they were seeing on TV. From their perspective, it all started with news about the raid, followed by news about Mr. Dupree's arrest, followed by the funeral service of a man who walked into the sanctuary alive, followed by different video recordings of people claiming to be healed, others claiming to be touched by invisible hands, and still others claiming to have seen a stranger who suddenly disappeared from them. More people came into the sanctuary. The crowd was beginning to get difficult to control. Pastor Matthew had no idea what to do next. He called Mr. Smith and Mr. Jones and asked them to help figure out what to do in the event the service continued throughout the night. His suspicions were spot on. The services continued well into the night. All night long people came in to pray, to sing, to worship, and to call on the name of the Lord.

The following day didn't experience any let up. More people came in to worship the Lord. Throughout the day they saw visitors from neighboring towns and from neighboring counties walk into the sanctuary. They were surprised by the deep sense of divine reality engulfing the building. The presence of the Lord was in that place. The meeting continued well into the evening. Pastor Matthew needed a break, but he couldn't leave the sanctuary. Sharon rushed home and brought him something to eat. After grabbing a bite in his study, he went back to the sanctuary to minister to the needy. More and more people came. In fact, the same trend continued into Friday and Saturday. Louella never missed a day of the revival. Except for Saturday when he had a wedding planning gig, Sam stayed in the sanctuary throughout. It was the most profound spiritual experience he'd ever had, and he was glad to have been a part of it.

Ironically, the crowd thinned out considerably on Sunday. The explanation was simple: Most of the believers who attended the revival wanted to worship in their home churches. Pastor Matthew sighed with relief. He was getting overwhelmed from not resting. That Sunday, however, the attendance at Rockville Community Church was much higher than previous Sundays. Most members came to see Rick Mulley and thank the Lord for saving him from the hand of death.

Pastor Matthew didn't have time to prepare his sermon that day, but he opened his Bible and landed on Romans 8:28: "And we know that in all things God works for the good of those who love him, who have been called according to his purpose." He traced the series of events from the time Louella lost her business, to the time Rick was supposed to have died, to the raid at Action News. He talked about how he felt the urge to pray for Louella when she was in the hospital and how he prayed for Jason when, at that very hour, Jason's car was soaring over a cliff and crashing forty feet below. All these were orchestrated by the Lord, Pastor Matthew argued, in order to bring people to repentance and to witness a visible demonstration of his presence. All in all, he closed the sermon with the following words: No matter what happens, God will always ensure that good triumphs over evil. The congregation stood up and gave the Lord a round of applause that lasted for nearly three minutes as some shouted words of praise to the Lord while others shouted "Amen" repeatedly. He then invited Mr. Smith to lead in the closing hymn for the day. What a week that was!

41

WHEN THINGS SETTLED, LOUELLA's business was restored. Her insurance covered the cost. It took about four weeks to repair the damage. She finally returned to her familiar routine and was able to touch base with the assistant she wanted to interview. Because of what happened to her business, more citizens of Rockville came to know about Rockville's Finest Flowers. They made it their shopping stop for their flower needs.

Sam continued with his wedding planning gigs. His relationship with Louella evolved into something deeper. They began courting seriously. Louella helped disciple Sam into a mature Christian believer. He became active in Rockville Community Church and joined a men's group, which further enhanced his faith as a disciple of Jesus Christ. After several months of courtship, he and Louella were engaged.

Rick Mulley got his job back as a detective with the Rockville Police Department. Thankfully, there were many police officers who didn't buy into their former boss's game plan. They remained loyal to the cause and honored their role as men and women in uniform. Rick was received with much jubilation. The community in Rockville respected him as a law enforcement officer. He, too, remained active in his church but, as before, maintained a very low profile.

Chief Drake Riley was relieved of his duty and incarcerated for his corrupt deals. He wasn't alone. The remaining officers who raided the news station were also punished for their brutality. When he finished serving his time in jail, he returned to the Rockville community and became a security officer in the Rockville mall.

Larry and Hank were incarcerated for twenty years for breaking and entering. James Dupree was also charged in a court of law and found guilty of the attempted murder of a police officer, along with aiding and abetting.

He lost his business, his home, and all his friends and associates. He, along with Mason, wouldn't see the light of freedom for the rest of their lives with no possibility of parole. To all intents and purposes, his life as a free citizen came to an end. His attempt to take over Louella's home was declared null and void.

Pastor Matthew continued with his ministry at Rockville Community Church. Since the revival, several more revivals happened at his church, none of which were orchestrated by human effort. They simply happened. More and more people joined the congregation. They saw the need to begin a second service to cater to the overwhelming influx of more worshipers. Pastor Matthew became a respected leader in the community, and the city often invited him to their meetings for spiritual counsel. His wife, Sharon, stood by him consistently. Their two boys grew to become role models among the youth in their part of town. Pastor Matthew and Sharon couldn't have been prouder of them. For years to come, what happened in Rockville Community Church came to be famously known as the Rockville Revival.

www.ingramcontent.com/pod-product-compliance
Lightning Source LLC
LaVergne TN
LVHW050645100826
845148LV00011B/1985

9798385257904